THE DRAGON'S BACK

THE DRAGON'S BACK

Ian Barclay

eagle

Guildford, Surrey

For John and Ann

British Library Cataloguing in Publication Data
Barclay, Ian
  The dragon's back.
  I. Title
  823.914

  ISBN 0–86347–031–9

First published in Great Britain in 1991

Published by Eagle, an imprint of Inter Publishing Service (IPS)
Ltd, Williams Building, Woodbridge Meadows, Guildford GU1
1BH

Set in 11/12pt Century by Input Typesetting Ltd, London
Printed in Great Britain by William Collins & Sons, Glasgow.

Table of Contents

Chap 1 The Main Course   1
Chap 2 Hot Lobster Pâté   14
Chap 3 Pigeon in Red Wine   25
Chap 4 Boeuf en Croute   40
Chap 5 Old Peculiar   55
Chap 6 Coffee for Two   67
Chap 7 Bream à la Vendangeuse   75
Chap 8 Breakfast on the Balcony   89
Chap 9 "Five Spices" Powder   100
Chap 10 Oat Cuisine   116
Chap 11 No Lunch Today!   121
Chap 12 Flowery Waists   132
Chap 13 Fast Food   143

Chapter 1

Just north of Brighton, beyond the Downs and nestling in a fold of the hills, lies Kings Nympton. It is to the West of the A23, beyond Herodsfoot but not quite as far as Hawkspeare. It is one of the oldest villages in Sussex. Its origin goes back to the days when most of the land south of London was a vast forest of oak. The trees of both the Sussex and Kentish Weald have long since been cut down, either to build the first vessels of a once mighty navy, or to provide fuel for the host of small businesses that always abound where there is a cheap supply of wood. Indeed the best known building in Kings Nympton is the Old Shot Tower, itself a relic of the days when the abundance of local wood kept the gunsmith's forges burning. Today it is known as *The Old Nail Shot Restaurant* and it is the reason why a tiny village, of no more than a handful of houses, is known throughout Sussex if not beyond.

A taxi pulled away from the seventeenth century cottage next to the restaurant. Mike Main, the restaurant owner, dressed in a crumpled linen suit, had jumped out with two large cases and a package. He fitted his key into the lock of the front door and let himself in. As he moved from the small hallway into the spacious sitting room there was a thud. For him the initial sensation was audible rather than tactile, like someone hitting a heavy gong near the back of his head. His legs gave way and as he fell to the ground he lost consciousness.

When he came to, he found that he was lying in the doorway, half in and half out the sitting room. The reverberating sound had given way to waves of pain which moved upwards from the base of his skull. He was about to command his unresponsive limbs to get up when he heard someone at the door.

"Is anyone there?"

He slowly managed to climb to his knees, still holding the back of his head with one hand.

"Are you all right?" The question was asked by a slender young woman with shoulder length auburn hair who had rushed forward to help. Mike enjoyed the brief warm sensation of a familiar scent. Her close proximity after the long months of anguish leading up to his wife's death made him want to prolong the encounter. Their eyes met briefly, both coloured slightly and they quickly moved apart. They were standing in the hallway of the cottage. On the wall immediately behind them was a Little Adam mirror, the smoky threadbareness of its backing made it look misty in a certain light. It added to Mike's inability to focus.

As his head began to clear, Mike turned from the room and focused on his visitor for the first time. As a restauranteur he had often amused himself by trying to guess the occupation of his customers. Publically he said this was the *trivial pursuit* of the kitchen, privately he would insist that he found it as enthralling as a good crossword, adding that the clues once unravelled were just as obvious. Without at first being aware that he was doing so, he had started to read the clues presented by his visitor. She wore a pleated camel skirt with Blackwatch green. At her neck was a single string of pearls. "A schoolmistress," Mike Main quickly thought, "at an independent school."

Little was he aware of how accurate he had been. Anna Richardson was in her early thirties and taught art at the girls' school which stands immediately above the Marina at Brighton. Roedean's height above the sea gives it a spectacular view of the English Channel. Occasionally, on a clear day, the Isle of Wight could be seen in the distance. To the East the majestic rolling Downs harbour small towns and villages. While to the West, was the ugly urban sprawl of Brighton and Hove.

"Are you all right?" She asked the question again but with greater urgency.

Mike Main appeared to hear it for the first time.

"I must have interrupted a burglar."

"I saw your door open and stopped to ask the way." She became concerned by his appearance. "I think you had better call a doctor or at least sit down."

"I am fine. Please don't worry. Where did you want to get to?" As he took his hand from the back of his head he realised there was a small amount of blood on his fingers.

"The Manor. Major Bradford's house." Anna paused as if having to overcome some reluctance. "I really think you need a cup of tea. Why don't I make it while you sit down?"

"Now that's a good idea. I've just flown into Gatwick and for the last few hours I have been sitting on the plane thinking about a good cup of tea. The kitchen is straight through there beyond the sitting room," he pointed the way, "Someone should have put some milk in the 'fridge. I think you'll find my kitchen functions like most others."

Anna made her way through, while Mike carried his cases as far as the sitting room. Apart from his head which was still a little tender, he was beginning

3

to feel much better. He glanced around, noting that his pictures and few pieces of silver hadn't been touched. He went up the open staircase to his bedroom and then through to the other rooms to see if anything was missing. When he returned, they met at the bottom of the stairs. He took the tea-tray and carried it to the low table in front of the sofa. "Why don't we pretend I am still not quite better and ask you to pour?" Without waiting for her reply, he continued, "It is very strange but I don't think anything has been taken. The only thing missing is the package I brought from Hong Kong, which is silly, because it doesn't have any value."

Anna Richardson sat down on the sofa and started to pour the tea. She handed him a cup, "While I was in the kitchen I realised who you are. You run the restaurant here and write the cookery article in the Sunday paper." As she spoke, she was aware that you could put two English people into a room knowing that they would never speak, but add a little crisis or accident and that very Englishness that kept them apart, would melt instantly bringing them together as though they had been friends for sometime. How strange, she thought, that calamity is one of the best forms of introduction for the English.

"I'm Anna Richardson. I teach art. Major Bradford wants to see me. That's why I am in Kings Nympton."

As they enjoyed a cup of tea together their shyness disappeared as they continued to introduce themselves. Mike Main confirmed that he ran the restaurant next door and that his column *The Main Course* appeared in a Sunday paper. She discovered that his wife had recently died after a long illness and that a month ago he had set off on a package tour of the Far East which had concluded with a week at the Peninsular Hotel in Hong Kong.

She revealed that she taught history of art at Roedean and had done so since coming down from St Andrews. Her special interest was the English artists of the early twentieth century, particularly those associated with Brighton, such as the Ditchling Community. She enjoyed teaching in Sussex because in her free time she could continue her research and studies.

It was her special knowledge of Eric Gill, eccentric artist and engraver, that Major Bradford wanted to use. He needed her advice on a few drawings that he had recently acquired.

There was a natural break in the conversation. "I must go, I can see that you are much better. Your tan has returned. You don't look quite so pale as you did half an hour ago."

Mike Main led the way to the front door. When he stepped outside he saw that her car was pointing up the road towards Fulking and away from Brighton. "The easiest way to go", he said with a sweeping gesture, "is simply to drive around the Green. At the far end of the village don't take Henfield road but go back the way you came, up Kissing Tree Lane and just before the wood on the left you will see the entrance to the Manor. It's concealed when you come down the hill but quite easy to see as you go up." He walked around the car and helped her in. "Thanks for making the tea. Why don't you come to the restaurant one evening. Bring a friend and be my guests. That could be my way of saying thanks for being such a Good Samaritan."

"I might just do that," she called as she sped away.

He watched her as she turned at the church and came back past on the other side of the Green. She smiled and waved. He saw her eventually turn right at the end of the village and head up the Brighton road towards the Manor.

Kings Nympton is a compact little village, its size determined by the fold in the Downs. The buildings

5

sit on three sides of the Green suggesting that there must have been a cattle market there in earlier days. The main Henfield to Brighton road forms one side of the triangle and is known as Kissing Tree Lane as it passes through the village. The name comes from the tall elms and oaks that meet over the road as it negotiates Kings Wood. Once clear of the trees, the road circles May Hill and climbs over the Downs to Brighton. On Mike's side of the Green, the buildings shelter against the November gales and icy blasts of winter by having their backs tucked well into the Downs. They consist of a row of cottages, *The Old Nail Shot Restaurant*, Mike Main's house, the vicarage and the parish church of St Rumon's. On the other side of the Green leading back to the main road stand Mervyn Lyle's antique shop, *The Den of Antiquity*, followed by the village pub and a few more cottages.

The cottages were built with local flint cobbles and originally housed farm workers. They had now been remodelled, thatched and extended at the rear to make room for new kitchens and bathrooms. In the morning before the wives run their children to school, their husbands can be seen hurriedly driving to Hassocks to catch the commuter train to the City. In defence of their present owners, it has to be said that the days of the farm worker are over in Kings Nympton. The local landowners tend their own land with all the help of hightech farming.

Mike went back into his cottage and phoned the police to tell them about the burglary. They promised to come out straightaway to see him. He then sat at a small knee-hole desk in the sitting room where his housekeeper had left him one or two notes. His attention was immediately caught by an "at home" card from Major Bradford, dated for that evening. He recognised the Major's bold handwriting commanding "Drinks at 7.30". Finally he let himself out of the side

6

door and crossed to the restaurant, to see how his team had managed in his absence. He did this without any sense of urgency because he was still officially on holiday and had another week to go, which he was determined to enjoy to the full.

Several hours later, having showered and changed, Mike paused to adjust his tie in the mirror near the front door before setting out for the Manor. Major Bradford lived in a solid Georgian house with a Paladian façade immediately below May Hill. It looked northward across the Weald toward Gatwick. There is a story that the original owner deliberately set the Major facing away from May Hill because of its pagan connotations. That could well be, as in Sussex it is difficult to completely eradicate the earthy worship that has existed there since before Christian times. A footpath is clearly cut into the side of the Downs and runs from the top of May Hill through Kings Wood to emerge in the kitchen garden of the Manor. The original owner may have wanted to look the other way, but almost certainly his servants enjoyed the revelry around the May Pole. They probably even managed a little dalliance in the wood on the way down before serving their master's lunch, their sober expressions hiding the morning's escapades.

Mike Main parked his car on the gravel in front of the Manor. The number of cars and the general murmur of conversation made him aware that it was quite a large gathering. As he walked up the steps he realised that he hadn't seen most of his neighbours since his wife's funeral. Inwardly he hoped that the endless discussion about cancer wouldn't start again. The Major was standing near the front door having handed drinks to a couple who had just arrived. Mike realised that it must have been the rear lights of their

7

car that he had seen in the distance as he turned into Kissing Tree Lane.

"Ah, Main," boomed the Major, "come and have a drink. What would you like?" The Major stood tall and erect, condescension flowed from him like a tide. He spoke with the loud commanding manner which seems to come so naturally to the landed gentry. "Gin and Tonic please." Mike followed his host through to the crowded drawing room furnished with comfortable armchairs and old oak, every inch the country gentleman's home. Not many people were sitting down, most were standing in small groups talking. The walls of the room were bare except for one or two family portraits which, because of their likeness to the Major, were obviously Bradfords of earlier generations. The Major came back through the crowd with Mike's drink in his hand.

"There you are Main. I think you know everybody here except possibly Miss Richardson over there by the fire talking to the new vicar."

Until that moment Mike was unaware of her presence, as he turned she smiled and lowered her head in a brief nod of acknowledgement. She had obviously been back to Roedean to change. The Major continued, "How is the restaurant? Going well by all accounts."

"You ought to come sometime."

"Yes, I really must. Mind you, I don't care for all this nouvelle cuisine. Good honest food with no pretence and a bottle of claret is what I like."

"I think you will find we can manage that." More people had arrived so Mike excused himself, "I'll go and talk to your guests over by the fire." He made his way through the crowd towards the fireplace. As he approached, Anna said, "How nice to see you again Mr Main. Do you know the Vicar? He is telling me about your church. I understand it is unique."

"How do you do, Vicar." Mike Main found himself

looking at a slight, bespectacled figure with a clerical collar and a baggy grey suit. "I don't think we've met, you must have moved into the village while I was on holiday? When he took my wife's funeral, Canon Coleman told me he was leaving."

"How do you do." The vicar spoke in a slightly breathless way with a hint of an impediment. "I was just ex . . . explaining that St Rumon's is an early S . . . Saxon church with a four-gabled tower crowned with a sh . . . shingled roof." Although the vicar was now talking to both of them, he was looking at neither. His large watery eyes were permanently looking over the top left-hand corner of his spectacles and in the general direction of the light fitting in the centre of the room.

"I don't think I have ever heard of St Rumon" said Anna.

"St Rumon," the vicar continued "was an early Welsh saint of the general period of St Brannoc and St Necton. Their missionary journeys took them around Cornwall and Devonshire but St Rumon was the only one who actually came along the south coast to the old kingdom of Sussex. In fact Kings Nympton was the most easterly point of his travels."

Mike was intrigued by this piece of local history, "You obviously know the area well. Was your previous parish near here?"

"Oh no, my latest job was er . . . in a diocesan office in the North. Yes the er . . . the North." For the first time he was looking directly at both of them, but somehow he didn't sound at all convincing. "I think I must return to the vic . . . vicarage, if you will excuse me." He didn't wait for a reply but put a half empty sherry glass on an oak stool and hurried from the room.

"What a funny little man," said Anna. "It is not often you meet a clergyman who sounds so unconvincing. I wonder what he's trying to hide."

"We will probably never know." Mike watched the vicar hurrying away and then turned back to Anna, "You found your way all right this afternoon?"

"Now there's another funny thing. Your directions were marvellous. Thank you. But as I turned into the drive, the Major was just leaving. He said there was to be a drinks party here at 7.30 and suggested that I might come back at 7 and stay on for a drink. When I arrived, he showed me into the library and took two superb drawings from a portfolio which he said were by Eric Gill. He then asked me what I thought of them. I said they were magnificent but obviously forgeries. To say the least, he was very angry which I presumed was because he had just paid the earth for them. I'd been upstairs to tidy up before the others arrived and by the time I came down, he was venting his anger on the young man over there. I think I heard the Major say to him that the pictures would have to be done again.

"Wait a moment," said Mike, "I'm not following you. You said the pictures were superb. If they were so good, how did you know they were forgeries?"

"Well that's it. Technically they were brilliant, but several things were quite wrong. The first was the model. She is known to all who are familiar with Eric Gill and appears in some of his best life-studies and wood cuts. She was an American called Beatrice Ward and didn't come to England until 1925. Gill didn't meet her until the last few years of his life when he worked at Pigotts near High Wycombe, yet both the drawings were signed and dated "Ditchling 1912". Which was at least thirteen years before Eric Gill met her. However, the biggest give-away was not the model but the lettering at the bottom of the picture, which said "ARTIST'S MODEL FOR THE SONG OF SOLOMON". You see, apart from being a good draughtsman and sculptor, Eric Gill had a life-long interest in typography. He actually invented typefaces and his lettering was always immaculate. Eric Gill was not the creator of those drawings. Whoever was, managed to copy his style in the artwork but not in the lettering. Eric Gill couldn't have lettered as clumsily as that in a thousand years."

The young man came through the crowd towards them. So the conversation couldn't continue. "'Ullo Mr Main. Nice to 'ave you home. Plenty of cars outside your place every night. They obviously got on without you. If I was you I would check on your staff. In case some was on the make. Know what I mean?"

Mervyn Lyle was typical of many of Brighton's antique dealers. So many began as knocker-boys in the rural parts of Sussex. Their so-called business was to rob elderly cottagers of their only good stick of furniture or piece of Staffordshire. The furniture would be quickly and expertly restored and within a few days resold at a vast profit. A profit that the tax man wouldn't hear about. *The Den of Antiquity*, Mervyn's shop, stood on the other side of the Green almost opposite Mike's cottage. Its window display never changed and consisted of a few good pieces of eighteenth century furniture. If anyone enquired about their price, they would be told that the items weren't for sale. On the other hand the shop hardly ever had any customers except in the summer when a few Americans passed through the village in search of rural England.

For most, Mervyn Lyle's financial survival was a mystery, unless they happened to be up early on a Tuesday morning, at which hour they could see him loading half a dozen identical Victorian brass bedsteads into a van in time to catch the early ferry from Newhaven. The remarkable feature about this operation was that each bedstead was identical down to the last minute scratch and dent.

Mike Main ventured a straw in the wind. "Merv, I've been meaning to ask for sometime. Do you ever deal in pictures . . . drawings?"

"What? Art Mr Main? Now you know me? A bit of furniture or a house to be cleared that's what I do. But your actual pictures? No. My friends wouldn't fancy it if I went all arty. Not my style is it?" With that he wandered off.

"What a strange chapter of events," said Anna, turning back to look at Mike. "A burglar, a mysterious stolen package, forged drawings, a not very convincing vicar and an antique dealer who is not telling the truth. You did say the package wasn't valuable? Did you mean that?"

"Yes, it was a vase I bought in Hong Kong. The communists have one or two shops where they sell things from mainland China. The one by the old ferry terminal in Kowloon has an antique department. I don't think the things are really old, they just look old. I saw what they call a beaker-vase, it had a striking blue pattern, and I bought it to make into the base for a lamp. It is a mystery why anyone would want to steal it. There must be a hundred things in the cottage that are much more valuable." He took the empty glass out of her hand, "Another?"

"No, I don't think I will thank you. I'd better get back to Roedean. When the girls are away I like to make the most of the peace and quiet to catch up on a bit of work." She smiled as she spoke.

"Let me take you to your car," said Mike. On the way out they both thanked the Major. He said how grateful he was for Anna's advice and mumbled something about the Brighton antique trade having too many rogues. As he said this, he appeared to be looking for Mevyn Lyle who had conveniently vanished. They walked down the mellow stone steps of the Manor, and as Mike held the door of her car open he said, "Do you think your mountain of work could allow you to have lunch tomorrow?"

"I would love that. I need an incentive to keep going."

"That's marvellous. Why don't we meet outside Hatchards at 12.30?"

"Until 12.30 then, goodbye."

A few minutes later Mike drove home. He felt weary after the long flight and the extraordinary events of the day. He had promised himself a crash course on how to live as a bachelor but wondered if this might be complicated by Anna Richardson. His car almost drove itself down Kissing Tree Lane and along the edge of the Green. The restaurant car park was still full. He garaged his car and as he approached his front door, all the events of the day came tumbling back into his mind.

He paused outside the cottage listening for the slightest noise. Away in Kings Wood an owl hooted mournfully. In the alley behind the cottages a courting couple knocked over a milk bottle and it clattered to a standstill. A door banged somewhere. A cat screeched at a hidden foe. From the village pub came the sound of a tinkling piano and a sudden burst of laughter. In fact, all the normal sounds of a Sussex village.

He put his key into the lock and let himself in. He felt for the light switch in the sitting room and switching it on saw, there in the middle of the sofa table, the package that had been stolen. It didn't look as if it had been touched. It was still wrapped as it had been in Hong Kong.

Chapter 2

North Street, West Street and East Street mark the outer edge of the little eighteenth century fishing village of Brighthelmstone. The fact that most of its inhabitants were sea-faring fisherman probably accounted for the lack of imagination in the choice of street names. Within the space bordered by these three roads and the sea lay a mass of tiny cottages linked by an intricate pattern of lanes and alleyways. Some have unfortunately been swept away by developers and even those that remain have been restored, pedestrianised and now house a number of small businesses, boutiques, wine bars and gift shops.

Brighton has prospered since the day early in the eighteenth century when Richard Russell, a doctor from Lewes, published his theory on the benefits of drinking and swimming in seawater. The good doctor was wise enough to invest in a few properties himself and so enjoyed the benefits of the building boom which he started.

Market Street is the least spoilt of the Lanes. Today, it is still possible to detect a fisherman's cottage hiding behind a modern shop exterior. Hatchard's bookshop is near the beginning of this small thoroughfare, immediately behind Hanningtons department store. On the dot of 12.30 Anna emerged from the rear entrance of Hanningtons and crossed over to Mike Main, waiting outside the bookshop. "Am I late?"

"No. Exactly on time."

"Good."

"So to my favourite lunchtime watering hole." Mike took Anna by the arm and steered her up Market Street past several small bistros, already buzzing with lunchtime activity. At Brighton Square they turned towards East Street and found themselves outside English's Oyster Bar.

"When you said a watering hole I was expecting a pub."

"Well I thought something a little more salubrious was needed." He held the door for her. However, their arrival had been noticed and a waiter took charge and ushered them inside.

Faded gentility would be a much better description of Englishes. The Oyster Bar forms the narrow entrance that leads into the main dining room decorated with Edwardian murals. As a restaurant today, it doesn't rate highly in the good food guides much to the delight of the regulars as this helps it keep the crowds away.

The bar stools are the front row of the stalls for the daily spectacle of the *maitre écailler* deftly going about his work. Selecting a native Colchester oyster from the tub on the bar he takes it with the care of the craftsmen about to work with his favourite material. To avoid spilling any of the precious liquid he holds it in a flat napkinned hand slipping a wide bladed knife under the hinge and with a easy twist the oyster is laid bare for all to admire and enjoy.

Local gardeners will tell you that the number of discarded shells must be evidence of the enjoyment of the oyster since time immemorial. An archaeologist could be more exact, asserting that these tasty morsels have been relished on the coastal plain below the Downs since neolithic times.

Mike helped Anna onto a bar stool and then took his place beside her. It occurred to him that there was an important question he hadn't asked. "I hope you like fish?"

"Well, it is not my favourite food. School kitchens always manage to spoil it. I think this is what has put me off in the past. But I'm sure I will enjoy it today."

Mike opened the shining red menu. "How about some oysters? You won't find any better than those." He pointed to the shallow wooden tub on the counter, "There's the genuine article all the way from Colchester."

"No, I don't think so. I'm not going to be quite that brave. Are you going to have some?"

"No, my favourite lunchtime meal here is hot lobster pâté. It's delicious."

"Why don't I have that too?"

"Well I *think* you will enjoy it."

By this time the *maitre écailler* was standing ready to take their order. "Have you decided Mr Main?"

"Yes, I think we have. Two hot lobster pâtés please and a bottle of Chablis. You know the one I enjoy."

"Certainly Sir, the Simonnet-Febvre."

"Exactly."

The bar was still relatively empty as the one o'clock rush hadn't started. At the far end a gaunt man was sitting very much by himself. His spartan meal consisted of half a dozen oysters, a single piece of french bread and a small bottle of Perrier water. By contrast, next to him were two Americans who were exciting their own gastric juices by reading the menu to each other. Occasionally this was punctuated with "Hey . . . how about this" followed by the ingredients of a particular recipe.

Anna hadn't really noticed the other people in the

bar. Simply seeing Mike again and recounting the events of the previous evening were enough to keep her mind occupied. "Do you know I actually dreamt about the Major last night? He was surrounded by a whole room full of forged drawings." She paused to reflect. "But I expect everything that happened last night had a perfectly logical explanation and there was nothing suspicious at all."

"Oh, I don't know" said Mike, conveying his own sense of doubt. "When I got home, the missing package had been returned. Something is wrong but I can't put my finger on it."

"What shall we do?"

"I'm not sure, that's the trouble. I still have a few days holiday left. I think I'd like to spend a little time just nosing around." He took a used envelope and a pen from the inside pocket of his jacket. "Why don't we list the things that were obviously wrong last night. That would be a good start."

"I suppose we have got to begin with the Major. He started the chain of events by inviting me to Kings Nympton to look at the drawings. And then there was the young man in antiques. The one who was on the wrong end of the Major's anger."

Mike Main started to write on the back of the envelope but then hurriedly crossed it all out. "I find it difficult to believe that the Major could be involved in anything sinister. He may have a blustering manner, but he is well liked in the village. His family have lived in Kings Nympton for years. What could be the motive? He is a wealthy man and could afford to throw away any number of forged drawings and buy a dozen genuine ones. It doesn't make sense."

Anna was still reflecting on the events at the Major's. "I felt there was something odd about the vicar. He seemed to be trying to hide something."

"I think we are going about this the wrong way,"

said Mike. "The key event last night was the burglary at my cottage, and it can't have been a random break-in because the vase was returned. The break-in made us suspicious even before we got to the Manor. I have a feeling that somebody there was linked to the robbery. Who better than Mervyn Lyle? Everybody knows he is a rogue. He left before we did which would give him time to put the vase back."

The waiter had returned with the bottle of Chablis and poured a little of the hay-green wine into Mike's glass. Mike savoured its bouquet and dry flinty taste before nodding that it was acceptable. Both glasses were filled and they had started to enjoy it when two plates of steaming pâté arrived. "I do hope you like this," said Mike. "If you don't, please say, and I will order something else. "I'm sure Carlos could persuade the chef to produce a steak."

Anna took a forkful of pâté and paused while she considered it. "Mmmm . . . actually it is *very* good. I don't think I have ever had a fish pâté before and certainly not hot lobster. I'm not sure what I was expecting, but it is *very, very* delicious.

Mike smiled in agreement.

The two Americans were determined not to miss anything. They had followed the arrival of the pâté and with a sense of expectancy and had waited for Anna to enjoy the first mouthful. "Gee, what a place." said the one wearing a rather bright Terylene blazer. and then, with the solemnity he might have used to announce that he was a member of the American Bar said, "I drive a Yellow Cab in New York. My hobby is food and wine. We have some great seafood restaurants in the U.S. But I tell you that *this* is something else."

Mike Main smiled. He hoped the Americans weren't going to be talkative but he didn't want to appear too stuffily British. "Now that *really* is a compliment. The

Oyster Bar in Grand Central Station takes some beating." He managed to say with a smile.

"Well, I can see that you know my city sir. And you must have enjoyed the full-shore dinner which you can still buy there."

Carlos had moved up the bar. As soon as he heard a compliment he would start to preen himself in spite of the fact that he wasn't responsible for the cooking. With an up and down waving motion, that suggested the Americans should slow down and come to a halt he said, "Mr Main writes on food Sir. I am sure he knows the good places to eat in New York."

"Is that right?" questioned the American "Are you Michael Main who runs the restaurant near here?"

"Yes, I am."

"Well, I read your column. It is syndicated in a lot of our papers and I use your recipes. We were actually hoping to get a table for dinner there one night. Is that going to be possible?"

By this time Mike was becoming slightly worried that the intrusion might stop him enjoying Anna's company. He assured the Americans that he would make a table available for them. With this both couples returned to the serious business of the food in front of them.

It wasn't until the coffee had arrived and the tourists had left with the inevitable "Have a nice day!" that the conversation returned to the original topic. Mike Main said "I think I'm going to try and see Mervyn Lyle this afternoon. Why not join me? Are you free?"

"Yes," said Anna, "But I have to get back to Roedean before five because I need to put some exam papers into the office to be typed."

"Well, we'll take my car and I'll have you back in Brighton by four."

They walked together through the Lanes and down to the seafront. The tiny thoroughfares were crowded with visitors who all seemed intent on finding a bargain. In reality few were to be found. But the charm of the place and the carnival atmosphere made many buy things they would never use.

In one square a student was playing a just recognisable version of Mendelssohn's Violin Concerto. While in another, a group of Americans stared at antique jewellery confusing themselves by trying to convert pounds to dollars using yesterday's formula for exchanging lire to francs. Everywhere there were language students, empty coca-cola tins and polystyrene boxes bereft of hamburgers and french fries. A student was sound asleep in a doorway. His bright red sweatshirt emblazoned with Macdonald's double golden arch, but underneath the logo, in the same style, it said "Marijuana". It was a cloudless day. The sky a flawless roof of the brightest blue with the sunlight shimmering on the sea. As they left the noise of the Lanes, Anna said, "Peace at last".

"Yes, it is much quieter here isn't it? Brighton is certainly a noisy old lady but I love her. She has everything I enjoy about a town, even if it is good to escape and live in the country." Mike suddenly came to a halt and said "Here we are". They had reached the car.

They quickly made their way through Brighton and were soon descending Kissing Tree Lane with Kings Nympton in the sunlight below.

Anna took in the panoramic view across the Weald as far as the eye could see. The horizon had just started to smudge with the first hint of a heat haze. She turned and said "You don't talk much about food do you?"

"Now that's an interesting thing." Mike adopted a thoughtful expression. "I wonder if miners talk about mines or if bricklayers always go on about bricks. Why do people expect a restaurant owner to talk about food?

Anyway I'm on holiday." He said this as if that settled the argument.

It didn't for Anna "It's not just the restaurant, you also write about food or have you written all the columns already?"

"I wish I had, I try to keep about three weeks ahead. I have a piece simmering at the moment, sometime today I must put pen to paper."

"What is it going to be about?"

"Salads."

"Oh, come on, you can't write about boring old salads in a Sunday paper. What will you say?"

"The art in writing a food column is to be practical and interesting. Salads aren't boring. Gertrude Stein said 'Roast chicken is roast chicken is roast chicken' – now that's boring, but salads have an endless variety of things to write about. You could start with the different ways lettuce was served to the Persian kings in the sixth century B.C. You could tell the history of salads in England, beginning with the first recorded recipe created by Richard II's chef in the 1390's. Or you could write a whole article on the new vegetables available in the supermarkets – celeriac, christoph-enes, rettich, salisfy." As they swung into his gate and parked the car, he turned and grinned, "Don't let me start or I'll never stop."

Anna laughed.

They walked across the Green towards Mervyn Lyle's shop which consisted of two large bay windows divided by a central entrance. In one window was an eighteenth century wheelback chair and in the other a Charles II gateleg table of the previous century. Both pieces were lit by an array of spotlights. Behind the window space was a heavy curtain which had the effect of concentrating the eyes on the display, concealing what was happening in the rest of the building. Above the shop a sign in large gothic letters declared *The*

Den of Antiquity and underneath in a much smaller type, 'Fine Antique furniture – proprietor Mervyn P Lyle.'

Between the shop and the row of cottages was Squeeze Belly Lane, said to be one of the narrowest passageways in England. Originally its incapaciousness was a builder's mistake. However, the villagers used it to their advantage in the bygone days of smuggling. A man, they would relate, could run the whole length of the lane carrying a cask of brandy without grazing his knuckles on the rough flint walls. By the time the Excise men had put their muskets down and shed their equipment to get through the lane, the brandy was already out of their reach and being enjoyed.

The side-door of *The Den of Antiquity* was near the beginning of the lane. By the doorway was a small window which was normally used for displaying some small objet d'art.

As Mike and Anna approached the shop they caught sight of a hurriedly written note pinned to door. Its message was concise, "Back Soon, M Lyle."

"Well, he can't be far away, his car is still here" observed Mike.

"He could be taking a late lunch."

"He might be doing something in the workshop at the back. Isn't that hammering?" They paused and a faint but regular tapping could be heard coming from inside the building. "It sounds as though he's making a few more genuine Victorian brass bedsteads." Mike didn't bother to explain the joke. "Let's try the side door."

As they stepped into Squeeze Belly Lane Mike came to a sudden halt and stared into the side window. "Well I never." Gone were the desk sets, and brass paraffin lamps and other bric-a-brac. In their place was a group of four Chinese vases, all in white porcelain with a rich cobalt blue underglaze. A show card standing to one side said "Rare K'ang Hsi beaker vases circa 1662 £100 each."

They looked at the vases in silence. "That's the sort of vase I have. Well, one like it. You can buy them in Hong Kong for £20. They are obviously not K'ang Hsi period, if they were, they'd be worth thousands."

They quickly strode to the side door and rang the bell. The hammering could still be heard and continued in a slow methodical rhythm. Mike Main was about to knock when he realised the door wasn't firmly shut. As he touched it, it swung open. It was easier to hear the tapping now.

"Merv, are you there?" he called.

There was no answer.

"Merv, are you at home?"

They made their way through to the rear of the shop. It was dark. The thick curtain acting as a backdrop to the windows prevented the sunlight from penetrating the workroom. The floor was littered with pieces of furniture in various stages of renovation. The knocking sound continued. It appeared to come from a small office at the back of the building. Negotiating a limb of a dismembered refectory table, they stepped into a room where the sun shone through an uncurtained window.

A man was lying on the floor. He had been shot. Blood was seeping through his shirt. Somehow he had managed to get hold of a walking stick and was hitting the uncarpeted floor in an attempt to get help. Mike recognised him as Mervyn's assistant and rushed forward. "Malcolm... you're hurt? What happened?" Kneeling, he managed to lift him to a sitting position. "Tell me what happened?"

"Mr ... er ... Main. A man from the ... er ... Typing ... Sss ... ss." The final sibilant became a long sigh and his head slumped forward onto his chest.

A trickle of blood dribbled from the corner of his mouth.

"He's dead."

The fact that the knocking had ceased emphasised the silence, which was suddenly broken by a door slammed somewhere in the building, a car engine roared into life and with screeching wheels sped away.

Anna stood pale and shaken while Mike gently laid the dead man on the floor. "I'd better call the police, there must be a phone somewhere." He quickly located it and switched a light on. The emergency operator connected the police who promised to be on their way immediately.

"Who did it, and why?" said Anna.

I don't know, but I think it means we have come to the right place. Only we are too late and should have thought about it earlier." After a pause he added, "The police will get to the bottom of it I'm sure. It looks as if Mervyn killed him. That was his car outside when we arrived. And that could have been him leaving in a hurry just now . . . we could check to see if it was his car speeding away?"

The main door of the shop was secured with a heavy chubb lock and there was no key. They used the side door again. As soon as they reached the top of the alley it became obvious that Mervyn's car had gone. With a shrug, Mike turned back to Anna, "Well, there we are. What an awful thing . . ." He didn't finish the sentence. Over Anna's shoulder he could see that the window for displaying objets d'art was empty. The K'ang Hsi vases had disappeared.

The siren of a police car could be heard in the distance.

Chapter 3

By late morning the following day, Kings Nympton had returned to some semblance of normality. The village was quiet once again. The press and the TV crews had got their pictures and filed their stories. The young City gentlemen were trading briskly on the financial exchanges and commodity markets. Schools and au pairs were occupying the young in their different ways. The wives were in Brighton at *Top Knots* for a shampoo and a gossip. On their way home they would do a mammoth shop at Waitrose. Golfers were teeing off at The Dyke for a round of the Scottish torture. Gardeners were getting out their trugs and kneelers and viewing the next crop of weeds to be tackled.

In an unmarked police car, Detective-Sergeant Percy Williams was about to call on Mike Main. He got out of his car and looked around in a slow and deliberate way. He was a lugubrious young man who had the idea that a serious manner added weight to his character. In reality it made him completely humourless and quite out of place in a fast moving community like Brighton, which is probably why his superiors had sent him to Kings Nympton.

"Do come in", said Mike. "I've just put the coffee on.

Why don't we go through to the kitchen and have a cup?"

"How kind sir," said the Detective-Sergeant, "I could do with a spot of motion lotion to get me going this morning. It is good of you to see me. I gather you know my boss. He suggested that you could help us."

Mike had learned not to talk about his customers. So he simply mumbled in a cautious way, "I think I do."

"At the moment Sir, we are looking for a little background information about Mr Mervyn Lyle. We want to know how the locals regard him? Does he fit in well with village life? What does he *really* do? I expect you know the sort of thing we want?"

Mike thought carefully before answering "If I say he is a bit of a rogue you will get the wrong impression. I am sure he pretends to be a greater villain than he actually is. In the pub he often jokes about retiring to Spain and calling his villa *DUNROBIN*. He comes from the East End and in a perverse way thinks its glamorous to be on the wrong side of the law. He certainly knows about antiques. When he clears a house he seems to have a sixth sense for spotting the important piece of furniture or china. Mind you, he is not against faking a regular supply of old furniture. That's what the old shed is for at the bottom of his garden. His roguish character is larger than life and the villagers love him for it." Mike paused "Everybody presumes he shot Malcolm. It *really is* quite out of character. He is not violent, even if he is a bit of a crook." As an afterthought he added "Have you found him yet?"

"I can't comment I'm afraid Sir. Except to say he is still missing and so is his car." The sergeant dropped easily into the jargon of his job. "We would like him to help us with our enquiries. But he is not in his usual haunts so we expect he has gone to ground somewhere. Does he have er . . . a particular lady friend locally?"

"Not in the village. He seems to have an endless supply in Brighton. Which he changes more often than the furniture in his shop."

"Yes, sir, we gather he is a bit of a lad." A flicker of a smile crossed the sergeant's face for the first time "We thought he might have a special girl friend somewhere in the vicinity."

"Not that I am aware of."

"Mmm." The sergeant appeared to have come to the end of his questions. "Is there anything else you would like to say that might be apposite?" he added in his most ponderous manner.

"I don't think so."

"Well, thank you, Sir." Still talking like a policeman he rose to his feet. "If you hear anything that would help us with our enquiries, I would be grateful if you would get in touch with us at Brighton Police Station."

Mike promised he would and then led the way out of the kitchen.

Having said goodbye he was about to close his front door when Anna sped past in her car. She saw him, braked and parked a little way up the road and came back towards him. "I thought we were going to meet at the pub?"

"We were. I got held up with a policeman."

"Have they found Mervyn Lyle?"

"Not yet. He seems to have vanished into thin air. Why don't you leave your car where it is and we could walk across to *The Slug and Lettuce*?"

Anna looked across the village green towards the pub. "Yes why not."

The Slug and Lettuce stood next door to *The Den of Antiquity*. The car park was already full. The combination of real ale and good food had made it popular. The village wives helped produce the food creating a thriving cottage industry. It was originally two small cottages which had been turned into a single building. The bar occupied the whole length of the ground floor and somehow managed to preserve a homely atmosphere. Good beer, wine and food was the only concession made to the twentieth century. The sound of electronic music and the clatter of computer games were conspicuously absent.

The publican, Max Keating was the son of a Brighton solicitor and sent down from Exeter University for attending neither a single lecture nor writing a single essay during his first year. On leaving home he discovered he had a temperamental disaffinity to any kind of work. Happiness for him was being with friends. So it was logical that he would invest an unexpected legacy in the freehold of *The Slug and Lettuce* when it came onto the market. Having once acquired the property, he set about re-fashioning it into the sort of place he would like to visit. The refurbishment was largely a matter of ambience and style. One noticeable feature of Max Keating's student days was a petite Welsh bombshell name Myfanwy. She had also failed her degree and had taken a job in the bar of the Student Union simply because she enjoyed the boisterous atmosphere of undergraduates. When Max Keating was sent down, he sensibly proposed to her and Myfanwy had become the life and soul of the public house in Kings Nympton.

Mike pushed open the bar door. The sound of conversation continued unabated. Most of the village seemed to have gathered for a lunchtime drink, standing in small groups discussing the murder and debating other great issues of life. The low beamed ceiling projected snippets of conversation from one end of the bar to the other. A flat Sussex burr said, "Well, I have heard they make their Best Bitter from potatoes, chemical and computers." An aspiring county inflection said "I don't like dogs, but I think I ought to have one. I'll have a lady dog." A chortle of laughter identified itself as coming from Belgravia. A South Coast cocky voice exclaimed "It really made my blood stand on end."

Max Keating had his back to Mike and Anna as they entered. He was holding a glass to the Gordons gin optic, pushing it firmly upwards to get a good measure. He saw them as soon as he turned back to the bar, "Well, well the wounded warrior returns. I hope you liked our new welcome home scheme. By special arrangement every returning holiday maker receives their own bespoke blow on the head . . . just to make them feel at home."

"If that was your plan, it certainly worked." Mike remembered the pain and unconsciously lifted a hand to the back of his head. Turning to Anna he said, "This is Max Keating, he runs this disorderly house. Max, Anna Richardson."

They both smiled their hellos.

"Welcome to Kings Nympton. What can I get you?" As he filled their glasses he continued. "Something slightly odd has started to happen while you have been away. People keep seeing dwarfs in the village at night."

"Oh, come on Max you're making it up. This is one of your *tall* stories."

"No, I'm serious, ask the vicar over there, it was one of his church wardens who saw them last Saturday."

On hearing his name, the vicar turned to face them "Ah, Mr Main and Miss Richardson. Good afternoon, how are you today?"

"Well thank you."

"Vicar," said Max, taking the clergyman's glass and filling it without being asked. "I was saying that it was one of your wardens who saw the dwarfs last Saturday."

"That is quite correct Mr Keating. Ab... About 10.30 pm to be precise. As far as he could see there were th... three of them, all armed with pick axe handles. He was walking his dog under the trees in Kissing Tree Lane, so they didn't spot him."

"Do you really mean *dwarfs*? It must be a joke? A student rag?" Mike struggled to understand what he was being told.

"Well," said the vicar, adopting his usual conversational pose of looking over the top of his glasses. "I wish it was as h... harmless as that. My church warden said that they were squat shrunken persons. Undersized m... men about the size of young boys at a junior school. As they p... passed, he was definitely aware of an overwhelming sense of evil."

"The plot thickens" said Anna.

The shapely Mrs Keating came down to their end of the bar and Max introduced her. "Ma, this is Anna Richardson, a friend of Mike's."

"How do you do" she spoke with a mellifluous Welsh lilt. "Actually my name is Myfanwy but call me 'Ma', everybody does."

"The vicar was just telling us about the dwarfs. They sound quite horrible."

"Oh village women are petrified. I can tell you" She nodded in a knowing way. "We haven't told the police yet because they haven't actually done anything." She paused "Now that I am here what would you like for lunch? Today's specials are taramasalata with pitta bread or hot moule salad."

Lunch was ordered and the vicar retreated to the far end of the bar where a group of his parishioners were holding forth on the need to cut the village green more often. This raised the perennial question about who would do the cutting and who would pay for it. Max moved down the bar to join in the fray. By the time he rang the bell for last orders, a heated argu-

ment had taken place and a considerable amount of
alcohol has been consumed, which meant that no serious conclusions had been reached.

Mike wiped his mouth with a napkin and turned to
Anna "I enjoyed that, I hope you did?" Without waiting
for a reply he added, "You remember yesterday when
we found Malcolm, he tried to say something? There
were two words. One was 'Typing' and the other began
with an 'S'."

"I don't think I will ever forget. I've never seen
anybody die before. Its permanently imprinted on my
mind."

"I'd like to go into Brighton and make some
enquiries."

"What would you look for?"

"A typing agency? Obviously it would help if we
knew how many there are in Brighton." Mike paused
and looked around. "I think that is a copy of the Yellow
Pages over there by the 'phone. Excuse me for a
second."

He was already flipping through the directory as he
returned. "Well there is nothing under *Typing*," he
said. "Oh, here we are. They are all listed under *Secretarial Services*." He paused. "Mm . . . there are only
three that could possibly help us. *The Typing Society;
Typing Services*; and *Typing Success*. Let's go and see
if they can throw any light on Malcolm's death."

Mike was so caught up in the events of the previous
day's shooting that he was already moving towards
the door and had presumed that Anna would follow.
It hadn't occurred to him to ask her. Just as it didn't
occur to her to point out his omission. She smiled
gently at his impetuosity. They were soon heading
over the Downs towards Brighton.

The Typing Society was in Bond Street. Its not the
most appropriate name for a road which is typical of

many of the streets just off the centre of Brighton. One or two seedy antique shops rub shoulders with several small businesses selling cameras, brightly coloured stationery, leather goods, videos and menswear. One end of Bond Street touches the tawdry glamour of the provinces, while at the other, it trails off into streets of small dismal traders and take-aways.

Mike found the building they were looking for towards the smart end of the street and even more remarkably there was a parking space a little further on.

A glance through the window of *The Typing Society* revealed that the space previously occupied by a counter had been furnished as an office, with rather basic furniture. Seated behind a desk facing the window was a gentle matronly figure wearing country casuals and half-moon spectacles. As Mike and Anna entered she closed a file and putting it to one side said "Can I help you?"

"I er ... wonder if you could tell us about the ... er Society?" Mike was momentarily lost for words.

"Well, it depends on what you want to know." She said with a slight shrug. "We offer post-graduate courses for young secretaries. With a diploma for those who want to take it seriously. I suppose you could say we are a finishing school for PAs dealing with the social side of their duties as well as giving instruction in all the technology available today. Does that help?" She gathered a sheaf of loose papers together from her desk and deftly dropped them once or twice onto her blotter to square them off.

"I think we really wanted to know if you do ... typing for people?" Anna was hardly more successful at finding the right words.

"Yes, we type manuscripts" said the matronly figure looking towards Anna, but quickly turning back to Mike, and with apparent recognition, "I think I *know* you? Aren't you the gentleman who writes on cookery? We don't type small articles, only complete manuscripts and dissertations."

"Yes I'm Michael Main. We are trying to find someone who did some typing for a friend in Kings Nympton. Either Mervyn Lyle or Malcolm Thraxter, they're both in antiques."

"Well, I can say with some certainty we haven't done any work for Mr Lyle or Mr Thraxter. Indeed I'm absolutely sure that we don't have a client in Kings Nympton." As she was speaking she had removed her spectacles and laid them on the blotter in front of her. She opened a drawer and took out a business card. She stood, walked round from behind the desk and handed it to Mike. "I fear I can't help you Mr Main."

"Well, thank you for trying."

"Not at all. Perhaps we can have the pleasure of doing something for you in the future." She crossed to the door and held it open. "Good afternoon Madam. Good afternoon Sir."

The next port of call was *Typing Services* in Ship Street. As soon as they found the address it was obviously that they had gone out of business. The premises were empty, but not completely, as though someone had suddenly taken the items of value. The shop door was boarded up and the overnight wind had funnelled the rubbish from yesterday's trippers into a deep drift against it. The place looked abandoned. The plate glass window had become a hoarding for opportunist bill posters. In a variety of cheap dayglo colours they announced *"David Bowie – Live in Amsterdam"*. *"Rhythm King present Schooly-D"*. Mike and Anna went straight on to Preston Street to look for *Typing Success*.

Being slightly away from the centre of Brighton, it was much easier to find and there was a parking space immediately outside. A yellow sandwich board stood on the pavement declaring: *FULL SECRETARIAL SERVICES – INCLUDING TELEX AND FAX-TYPING OF EVERY KIND – PHOTOCOPYING*.

As Mike and Anna opened the door they stepped into a business being run in the most energetic way by two young girls. Their faces, figures, jeans and streaked hair were so similar they could easily be mistaken for twins. Their T-shirts were the only distinguishing feature. Both were from current West End shows, one had the wide feline eyes of *CATS* and the other less mysteriously said *LES MISERABLES*. *Les Miserables* was on the telephone but looked up as they entered and said "Shan't keep you a second".

The shop was cramped and untidy. Two typists desks faced the left-hand wall providing the space for the keyboards and the VDUs of two IBM Personal Computers. Both desks were cluttered with overflowing ashtrays, empty Marlboro packets, stationery and open files. A long narrow table against the rear wall supported the Fax machine and a Canon copier. The young girl in the *CATS* T-shirt was working the copier. The rapid flash of light under its top was followed by sheets of A4 shooting from one side and adding to a growing pile of copies. Everywhere was claustrophobically crowded, even the ceiling space had accumulated a heavy blue fug of cigarette smoke.

"OK. I've got that, you want one mail shot to everybody on both lists. . . . It will go tomorrow by the afternoon post at the latest. . . . Bye." *Les Miserables* put the phone down and looked up towards Mike and Anna. "Sorry about that. What can we do for you?"

"We are trying to find someone who has done some work for a Mr Mervyn Lyle or Mr Malcolm Thraxter", said Mike hesitatingly. He was again aware that he was not quite sure what they were looking for.

Both girls looked at each other and smiled. *Les Miserables* said "we both know Mervyn. But not in the area of work. It is normally in the evenings after we are closed, in the Clarence Wine Bar."

"Are you from the police?" interjected *CATS*. "There is a rumour that he was involved in a shooting."

"No, we're not" said Mike, "just neighbours. We're looking for him because we want to see if there is anything we can do."

"Sorry, I don't think we can help," said *Les Miserables*. "Mervyn Lyle is pretty persistent in the evenings. But it is only because he wants to date one of us. It never has anything to do with work."

"Well, thank you."

"Bye."

"Goodbye."

Once they were back in the car Mike said, "Well that's it. What do we do now? Those two obviously knew Mervyn Lyle but only in the sense that he wanted to be their inamorator. That's quite obvious."

"I don't know what to suggest."

"I have an idea," said Mike after a moment, "but it hasn't got anything to do with Mervyn Lyle. Let's go back to Kings Nympton and I'll cook a light supper and then we can plan our next move."

When they got back they enjoyed a quiet drink together in the sitting room of Mike's cottage. As he handed Anna a glass he said, "So *this* is your half term?"

"Yes, that's why I have a little free time. I had intended staying at school over the holiday. One day I would like to write a book about Eric Gill and I was planning to look around Prestonville to see where he was born." As she spoke she was aware that it might appear she had spent the last couple of days in Mike's company with some reluctance. Anxious to correct any misunderstanding she quickly added, "But I can do that some other time."

"I don't want to deprive the art world of a major new biography."

"Oh, I wasn't intending to write anything like that" she said with self-deprecation, "but if you study an artist especially in the area where he lived, you inevitably discover some of the forces that made him work in a particular way and the problems that gave texture to his art. I want to record these so that future generations don't have to look for them all over again."

"That would seem to me to be the basis of an important study. I don't want to stop you working on it."

Anna looked away for a moment because she was aware that what she was about to say would be more revealing than she cared to admit.

"I have *really* enjoyed the last two days. I wouldn't have missed them for the world. You said that you are on holiday until the beginning of next week. My half term finishes then too. If you can bear it, I would love to help look for Mervyn. The last few days have been a wonderful distraction from the demands of term time – a real adventure, not just a TV thriller.

Mike realised that the conversation was making him feel self conscious too. So he brought the subject to an abrupt conclusion. "OK Let's decide to look for Mervyn Lyle together, until we both have to return to work. Then we will have to leave it to the police anyway. Now, what shall we have for supper?"

"Are you *really* going to cook?"

"Of course."

"Then I think we should leave the choice to you. After all you're the expert," said Anna teasingly.

"My suggestion is pigeon in red wine with just a hint of chocolate in the sauce."

"Chocolate?"

"Yes, you'll see."

Mike picked up the telephone from the table beside the sofa. "Oh Sue, the kitchen please." After a pause

he continued, "I wonder if someone could bring the
ingredients for the pigeon across to the cottage? . . .
Yes, that is right, in the marinade . . . enough for
two . . . with some vegetables . . . whatever is really
fresh at the moment and a bottle of Vosne Romanée.
Thank you." He replaced the receiver and turned back
to Anna. "Now where do you suggest we start
tomorrow?"

"I have been thinking about that. When we made
the list in Brighton yesterday, we both put Major
Bradford at the top. Then you crossed him off. I think
we should try to see him. But we *must* be more certain
about what we are looking for. Certainly more than
we were at the typing agencies this afternoon."

"I agree. But what *are* we looking for?"

Anna frowned thoughtfully, "a link between the
Major and Mervyn? Something that is real enough to
account for robbery and murder?"

As they continued to make plans for the next day
noises came from the kitchen indicating that the
ingredients for their supper had arrived. By the com-
motion, it was obvious that two young people, probably
girls by the giggling, had crossed the dark garden from
the restaurant and had struggled to open doors while
carrying heavy trays. These were eventually clattered
down noisily on a working surface. Finally an outer
door was shut restoring peace and quietness to the
kitchen and cottage once more.

"Now let's make sure we have got this right," said
Mike fishing for a pen and a piece of paper from his
jacket and making notes. "We need to establish . . . a
business connection . . . between the Major and
Mervyn. Probably linked to a typing agency somewhere."

"If we could get the Major to admit he bought the
drawings from Mervyn that would be a start," said
Anna still in a thoughtful pose.

"Now let's leave all that until tomorrow and see what needs to be done about supper," said Mike as he stood and led the way. Anna had already seen the kitchen when she had made tea at their first meeting. Seeing it again she remembered how well the old ceiling beams and thick cob walls blended with the modern fittings, faced with seasoned oak. Small terracotta tiles covered the working surfaces and the fittings were all old brass.

Once in the kitchen it was obvious why the girls had struggled with the trays. Both were large and were heavily laden with everything necessary for supper; bowls contained all the food, together with the china, silver, linen and the bottle of wine had been opened to allow it to breathe.

Mike took charge immediately, lighting four or five rings of the hob and putting the potatoes on to boil.

Anna said "what do you do with the pigeon?"

"Take it out of the marinade first," said Mike fishing four pieces from the bowl of red wine, onions and fennel. He laid them on kitchen paper. "I'll dry them in a moment and fry them like steak. But I need to make the sauce before that." He took the handle of the smaller frying pans and ladled in some marinade.

"Sauces are difficult."

"This one isn't. Just a little of the marinade, half a square of chocolate and a teaspoonful of fruit jelly. All you have to do is to reduce it and you will have a delicious sauce. It has a chocolately richness that is just right with game."

Mike finished the sauce then fried the pigeon. The breasts were cut horizontally, creating four pink medallions of meat on each plate, and then covered with the vegetables and sauce. As they enjoyed supper in the sitting room, from trays on their knees, the food perfectly complemented by the full bodied burgundy, they settled plans for the next day. Anna would drive across to King Nympton mid morning and they would try to see the Major.

Later, as Anna drove home up Kissing Tree Lane, an owl from Kings Wood swooped low and was momentarily caught in the beam of her headlights. Higher up the lane she saw a pair of badgers out for their first nocturnal foray of the evening. The height of the bank, the narrowness of the lanes and the approaching car made them lean together with the ease and assurance of two grey-haired lovers. Life is so much simpler for badgers thought Anna.

Chapter 4

Next morning Anna retraced the route of the previous evening. In daylight everything was quite different. The sun was high and warm in the sky and huge white clouds brocaded the Downs with their shadows. The trees of Kings Wood were breaking into leaf with all the life-giving force of early May. Kissing Tree Lane was waking to the rich colours of summer. Every hue could be seen: campion red, buttercup yellow, with wild strawberry and woodruff prinking the dark undergrowth with white stars. Shafts of sunlight caught great banks of blue bells. It looked as though an artist had hurriedly shaded the whole area with a bright blue crayon. For those who knew where to find them, the rare colour of the early purple orchid could also be seen.

As Anna descended the hill to Kings Nympton, she again thought of badgers and the simplicity of pairing in the animal kingdom.

Mike opened the door of his cottage as she arrived. "I saw you coming. I've phoned the Major and he's invited us for coffee."

They set out immediately. On the way they reminded each other of the need to establish a definite link between the Major and Mervyn, one strong enough to account for the robbery and Malcolm's death.

As the car crunched to a halt on the gravel outside the Manor, Anna saw that the approaching summer was just as apparent in the Major's garden. The three or four horse chestnut trees that framed the house, had filled out in the last few days and become substantial spheres of foliage covered with candles of blossom. Somehow they managed at the same time, to look soft and fluffy in the breeze yet solid and immoveable on their short heavy trunks.

They rang the bell and after a few moments the door was opened by the Major himself. "Ah, come in both of you," he ushered them inside. "Now why don't you go in there," he pointed towards the drawing room, "and I will get the coffee."

There was hardly a pause before he came back carrying a tray set with cups and a cafetière. "I think it must be your influence Main. My Mrs Boxall is certainly on her toes this morning." The Major turned to Anna, "Would it be too much to ask you to deal with this?" He set the tray down in front of her just as Mike had done at his cottage and again Anna didn't feel that she could protest. The Major then chose a seat next to Mike. "I gather there is something that you want to ask?"

"Yes, you probably know that we found Malcolm Thraxter just after he was shot yesterday."

"I don't see how I can possibly help?" The Major peered over his steepled fingers as he tapped them together thoughtfully.

"No. Not with Malcolm's death . . ." Mike was about to continue when Anna, having taken a deep breath, plunged in.

"We think the drawings, Malcolm Thraxter's death and Mervyn Lyle's disappearance are all connected."

"If you will forgive me Miss Richardson, I will have

to repeat myself." The Major had ceased his pensive tapping. He had taken a cup of coffee from Anna and was now sitting well forward in his chair, ready to argue his case. "I can't see any possible connection between me and Mervyn Lyle, or Malcolm Thraxter. There is, of course, a link between me and the drawings. I acquired them and asked your advice. You are, after all, an authority on Eric Gill."

"I am not sure I would use the word *authority*. I am very interested in his work and know it well, but that is all." For a moment Anna seemed to have lost the initiative. But she quickly continued. "When people were arriving for drinks on Thursday I got the impression that you'd just bought the drawings from Mervyn Lyle. It seemed to me you were rather upset that they weren't genuine?"

"I think you must've got hold of the wrong end of the stick, Miss Richardson," the Major was quite emphatic.

"Well you were certainly talking to Mervyn as if you knew him well."

"Of course I know him. Most of us have lived in Kings Nympton for a long time. It is a very small village. I have bought pieces of furniture from him from time to time. Mervyn Lyle has even had pieces made for me. I think that's what you must have in mind, Miss Richardson."

"Anna" Mike turned to her, "the Major is right, I don't think we should pursue this."

Anna hoped that no-one had noticed her slight loss of composure when Mike had used her first name. He had used it, of course, when they were alone together, but she felt self-conscious hearing him say it publicly for the first time, which was obviously very silly.

"Well, I am not convinced" she managed to say.

"Anna" Mike spoke gently, "I think we should give

the Major the benefit of the doubt." He used her name again, but this time it didn't affect her.

"Thank you, Main" the Major was visibly relieved. He sat back in his chair and started to drink his coffee, "I thought I might try your restaurant tonight. Will you be there?"

"We haven't discussed this evening" Mike glanced at Anna and then back to the Major. "I thought we might go there, but Anna might have other plans." He turned to her, "What do you think? It is about time you saw the inside of *The Old Nail Shot.*"

"I don't think you should entertain me again."

"We will debate that some other time." Mike smiled, "I know you are free. So I suppose I ought to ask you if you would like to go there tonight?"

"I'd love to. I've been wanting to for some time."

"That settles it," Mike turned to the Major, "We'll be there. Would you like to join us?" If I ask for a table for 8.30, would that suit you?"

"How kind" the Major's whole personality had softened and he become almost genial. "More coffee?" he beamed.

"No thank you."

"Not for me"

"See you at 8.30 this evening," the Major stood, indicating that the interview was over.

Once outside they drove in silence to Kissing Tree Lane. Anna pulled into a parking area near the bottom of the hill, designed to give sightseers a view across the village. From this vantage point it was easy to see why Kings Nympton had won so many awards for the best kept village in the county. The lawns in each garden appeared like strips of green baize with neat flowerbeds. The paintwork and the thatching of the cottages sparkled in the sunlight and, in spite of the debate at *The Slug and Lettuce*, the village Green looked better kept than most pieces of common land.

Anna broke the silence. "I think you were right" she sighed. "There is no reason to believe that the Major was involved in Malcolm's death or Mervyn's disappearance." She sighed again, "So what do we do now?"

"I don't know. Back to our original list? Who was next?"

"I think it was the vicar. I thought he was trying to hide something." Anna wound open the car roof so they could enjoy the warmth of the sunshine.

"Well we could easily see him now, if he's at home. Why don't we try the vicarage to see if he's there. Then I think I must spend the afternoon working on an article. It will give me a good appetite for dinner."

"To the vicarage" said Anne turning the ignition key and bringing the engine back to life. They descended the last part of Kissing Tree Lane, turned left on the south side of the Green and headed toward St Rumon's vicarage.

The vicarage was a large red brick building standing in several acres of unfussy garden. The magnolia and lilac were already in bloom. Those who wished to be rude about the vicar's home normally put it in the architectural period known as *late-LCC*. That was before the abolition of the London County Council. Today a house agent would describe it as a desirable Victorian residence. Honesty ought to make him add that it looked slightly tired when compared with the cottages in the village which was rather surprising, because they were very much older. As a house and a parish office it was functional but far too big for the Revd Peter Hoskins and his wife. If they'd had a family it would have been a different matter; they didn't and even after their brief occupancy they were beginning to worry about the cost of heating and cleaning such a large house in the winter.

Anna parked her car next to the Vicar's small white Fiat. In white letters on a green sunshield across the top of the windscreen, it said *THE PARSON'S PANDA*. Anna thought it was a splendid piece of PR for a younger clergyman but somehow totally incongruous for the present incumbant of Kings Nympton.

A gardener was cutting the grass as they arrived. He didn't look up as they parked and crossed to the vicarage. He was dressed in jeans, western boots and a denim shirt. His hair was worn in the style made popular by John Lennon in the 1960s. It would have been easy to assume that he was doing a few odd jobs in return for enough money for a night's lodging. Whereas the truth was that the vicar had inherited him when he moved into King's Nympton.

He lived rough in the vicarage stables, having permanently laid out his sleeping bag on the hand-pulled hearse, which had been stored there for as long as people could remember. It was village property, but it hadn't been used since the early 1920s. One day it would find its way into a transport museum. On one side of the funeral cart, under the dust and bat droppings, it was just possible to see the royal coat of arms of George III. The gardener's real name was Harold Gittings, but the locals knew him as *Hallelujah Harry*. Born in Sussex, he had gone to San Francisco in search of drugs and happiness at the height of *Flower Power*. A rescue mission near Fisherman's Wharf found him after he had had a bad experience of drugs and nursed him back to health. Harry had never been bright and drug abuse had made him less so. So he had become a natural drop-out. Having found peace of mind at the revivalist meeting in San Francisco, he had come home to Sussex. He was a willing work-horse and was content to be the verger at St Rumon, church cleaner and a general odd-job man at the vicarage. Matins at the parish church was about as far as you can get liturgically from the mission on Fisherman's Wharf, but even a hint of Moody and Sankey, would set Harry rejoicing in a loud and unmistakable way – hence his name. On this particular day he hadn't noticed Mike and Anna's arrival and continued to cut the lawn, as the vicar answered the doorbell.

"Ah ... Miss Richardson and Mr Main. What can I do for you?"

"We wondered if we could have a brief word?" Mike was again conscious of the difficulty of finding a link, this time between the vicar and Mervyn Lyle.

"Of course ... my study is just there. The first door on the left." He directed them to an excessively untidy smallish book-lined room. An ancient Roneo duplicator took pride of place in the middle of the floor. It appeared to have been used recently but there was no evidence that it would ever be put away. The rest of the floor was covered with piles of hymn books, sheet music, bibles and a collection of cardboard boxes overflowing with items for the Girl Guide's next jumble sale.

On the mantelpiece, standing by itself, was a Chinese beaker vase with the tell tale cobalt blue underglaze of the K'ang Hsi period. Mike and Anna saw it at exactly the same moment. They glanced at each other. Mike turned to the vicar, "I bought a vase like that a few days ago in Hong Kong. Have you had yours long?"

"Only a day or two. M ... Mervyn Lyle gave it to Harry in return for some work. I have an interest in China. My parents were missionaries there. I wanted to follow in their footsteps, but the Communists put paid to that in 1949, but I did Chinese for my degree."

"*Harry* gave it to you?"

"No it would be unfair to take it from him. I paid him for it, so he could buy a new pair of jeans." He lifted the vase from the mantelpiece and was holding it in his hands as he spoke. "It is only a copy, of course and not as valuable as it looks." It was noticeable that once the vicar had overcome his nervousness he had also lost his stammer and stopped looking over the top of his glasses. "Now what can I do for you?"

"Actually it was about the vase," said Anna. "We feel that the recent happenings in the village – which include a vase similar to this – are connected with Malcolm's death and Mervyn Lyle's disappearance."

"Oh, surely not."

"Would you mind if we spoke to Harry on the way out?" Anna addressed the vicar as he replaced the vase.

"Do, but I'm sure that Harry has no connection with Mervyn's disappearance. He told me that Mervyn gave it to him for helping to load some heavy furniture into his van. And I saw him doing just that."

"Well we'll have a word with him as we leave if we may, he may have seen something." Almost as an afterthought, Mike added, "Has your churchwarden seen the dwarfs again?"

"I don't think so."

"There's a whole series of seemingly unconnected events but *somewhere* there is a connection."

"Are you sure, Mr Main?"

Anna turned from inspecting the vase on the mantelpiece. "We think so. That is what we are looking for. But how you find a link between a K'ang Hsi vase, a bunch of dwarfs and a murder I don't know."

"Miss Richardson, the dwarfs are a separate issue." The vicar spoke with conviction.

"How do you know?"

"Well, a man's been shot, mercifully that is quite a rare event in Sussex, whereas dwarfs traditionally belong to this area and are very much part of our history."

"Obviously, you know something we don't" Mike shrugged as he spoke.

"I thought it was well known that in the sixteenth

century Felix Platter made a fortune from selling dwarfs to the bands of travelling entertainers that roamed the country, as well as exporting them to most royal courts in Europe."

"Did . . . er he come from Kings Nympton?"

"No not Felix Platter. He came from the area. What came from this village was the formula for producing dwarfs."

"You're joking?"

"No. People like Felix Platter would buy small children from the very poor villagers at a price they couldn't possibly refuse. They would feed them with *hindering agents* or *dwarfing potions* that would stunt their growth and even stop them growing."

"And these potions came from Kings Nympton?"

"That's right."

"What were they?"

"Well, the full formula has only recently been rediscovered but it was there for all to see in literature and wild flower books."

"Well, it might be obvious to you vicar, but not to us. As they say – can you give us a clue?"

The vicar assumed a donnish pose. "Lysander referred to it in *A Midsummer Night's Dream* 'Get you gone, you dwarf, you Minimus, of hindering knotgrass made. You bead! You acorn!' "

"Knotgrass" said Anna who had been silent for the past few minutes.

"Exactly" said the vicar. "The juice of two common roadside herbs, Knotgrass, *Polygonum Aviculare*, and Dwarf Elder, *Sambucus Ebulus* were mixed with the milk of the common daisy *Bellis Perennis* and fed to the children. It was very successful in producing top quality dwarfs who were sold at hefty prices – giving people like Felix Platter their vast fortunes."

"How do you know this?" Anna was amazed at the vicar's knowledge.

"Well my hobby is the *flora* of Sussex. I've published one or two monographs on the subject. And it all ties in with recent discoveries about dwarfing agents."

"It is most interesting vicar. I can quite see why you don't think the dwarfs and the murder are connected. But they could be."

The vicar didn't answer but just beamed "I love 'Silly Sussex'. Silly that is *silag*. It is an Anglo Saxon word meaning *sacred*. Sussex is a very *special* place."

There was a natural break in conversation. Anna made a move. "You've been most helpful vicar. Thank you. If we may, we will have a word with Harry as we leave?"

They found him near where they had parked the car. He was just finishing a sweep of the lawn with the mower and was about to turn and start again in the opposite direction. It quickly became apparent that he had no connection with Mervyn Lyle apart from occasionally helping with a heavy load.

After leaving the vicarage, Anna dropped Mike at his cottage before going back to Roedean, her thoughts were on what she would wear later that evening. The badgers couldn't have been further from her mind.

It's difficult to be exact about the age of *The Old Nail Shot* buildings. About four or five centuries would be a conservative guess. The first builder must have been an ironworker who chose the site because of the availability of fuel. What became *Andreds-Weald* of the *Forest of Andred*, shortened over the years to *The Weald*, then covered much of Kent and Sussex.

The restaurant site could be divided into two. The side furthest from Mike's cottage was a car park. Then a small single storey building ran down to the road, which was where the gunsmith had housed his furnace in earlier days. This was now the foyer of the restaurant and had been furnished as a drawing room.

Running in a westerly direction, parallel with the road, was an old Moot Hall which was the restaurant's dining room. On one side this had an uninterrupted view of the Downs while on the other it overlooked the village Green. Separating the restaurant from Mike's cottage was a tiny stream that ran from the Downs.

Situated at the angle of the building, linking the foyer and the dining room, was the Old Shot Tower, where shot used to be manufactured. Today this was the Duck's Foot Bar, taking its name from one of the more famous guns produced locally. The *Duck's Foot* pistol, was a favourite with gentlemen in the latter part of the eighteenth century who carried it in their coaches to protect themselves against highwaymen and footpads. It had the advantage that it didn't have to be carefully aimed, simply pointed in the general direction of a marauder. If shot from one of the four splayed barrels failed to hit the target, the noise of firing normally sent the robber on his way leaving the occupants of the coach unharmed, and still in possession of their valuables. The Duck's Foot Bar was designed for customers who liked to sip a cocktail perched on a stool. A canopy in the shape of the pistol hung over the bar and if nothing else it provided a topic for conversation.

Just before 8.30 that evening, Anna parked and entered the restaurant. There were several small groups of diners in the foyer deep in conversation. The Major was seated at an otherwise empty circle of chairs near the door. He stood as Anna entered. At precisely the same moment, Mike appeared through the archway from the Duck's Foot Bar and came down the steps. With him were the two Americans that he and Anna had met in Brighton.

"Well, there's a perfect piece of timing", it wasn't immediately obvious whether Mike was referring to his own or to Anna's arrival. He turned to the Major,

"I've asked two visitors to join us. Major Bradford, may I introduce Mr and Mrs Lane from the United States."

For a moment it appeared the introductions were going to get off to a rather shaky start. The Major stiffened and appeared slightly thrown by this intrusion but after a brief moment his composure soon returned and he held out a hand, "How do you do Mr . . . er Lane, Mrs Lane."

"Oh come now sir that is a little formal for folk like us. Why don't we settle for Wayne and Chelsea-Ann?" The Major, however, attempted to hide his very British feelings on the matter.

Once the introductions were over Mike took orders for drinks which he passed to a young man who had appeared with a pile of leather-bound menus. Mike opened them and handed them around. Before he sat he said, "Now this is your first visit to *The Old Nail Shot*. I want it to be a memorable occasion so please order whatever you would like." The group was suddenly quiet as they started to reflect on the gastronomic options before them.

Wayne Lane broke the silence.

"Y'know Mr Main, seeing as Chelsea-Ann and I are strangers in these parts, I think we need your help. Is there a specialty of the house?"

"Everything is special" Mike smiled. "The fillet of *boeuf en croute* will be enjoyable or if you want something a little lighter there is a warm salad of Bresse pigeon. You could start with the smoked salmon which is produced locally just down the road at Edburton, or Gravlax and dill sauce."

Dinner was ordered. Most chose Gravlax. Wayne Lane went for the consommé with a side glass of Malmsy because he had never tasted Madeira wine. For the main course the Americans chose the *boeuf en croute* while the rest the warm salad of Bresse pigeon.

They were all seated in the dining room at a table

with a spectacular view of the Downs and well into the main course when Chelsea-Ann said, "We drove into the country for lunch today and discovered a pub called the *Mucky Duck* which I gather was originally the *Black Swan*. When did your pubs get these crazy names?"

"Oh, they go right back in history" said Anna.

"Do you mean back as far as the days of Queen Elizabeth like this room?"

Nobody appeared to answer. So Mike said "Roman times would be much nearer the mark."

"You're kidding?"

"No there's evidence that the Romans used to hang a bunch of vine leaves outside an inn, so that the soldier could spot it easily. That seems to be the origin of pub names with a 'bush' in them, like 'The Old Bull and Bush'."

"Hey Wayne did you hear that? These pub names are real pieces of history."

"If it wasn't the Romans who started it, it was the Saxons a few hundred years later. 'The Pig and Whistle' comes from the Saxon word for bucket, *piggen*. In those days ale was served by dipping your mug straight into the host's bucket. And *wassail*, a toast meaning 'be of good health!' So 'Pig and Whistle' used to mean 'here's a bucket of good health' – just as you say, 'here's mud in your eye'."

"Well, Well" said Chelsea-Ann, "And I thought history was as dry as old boots. Did I hear, Mr Main, that you have been robbed and found a body?"

"That's right. But both didn't happen at the same time. As the Major knows." Mike turned to bring the whole table into the conversation. "Anna and I are trying to find the connection between the two events."

"Is that right?" Chelsea-Ann could make the shortest word sound as though it had several syllables.

"Yes, if you can tell us the connection between K'ang

Hsi vases, a murder and some dwarfs, we would be very grateful."

"What kind of vase?" Everybody was now caught up in the conversation between Mike and Chelsea-Ann.

"K'ang Hsi. It is er . . . a vase with a bright blue underglaze. From the K'ang Hsi period in China."

"I'd love to see one."

"That isn't too difficult. Mine is in the cottage. We could pop in after dinner."

"Oh dear, Wayne and I will have to hurry off then."

"I could get it now."

"Would you *really*? I would *love* to see it", said Chelsea-Ann innocently.

"Would you excuse me for a moment" Mike glanced around the table. "Chelsea-Ann wants to see the vase. I thought I would get it from the cottage." Mike left the table and went out of the door that led to the kitchen and then through the side door into the garden. It was quite dark and easy to see why the two girls had difficulty with their trays the previous evening. Mike made a mental note to do something about the lighting.

He quickly found the vase and was returning to the restaurant. This time the even brighter light of the cottage kitchen made the darkness of the garden more difficult. Mike thought for a moment that he saw a shadow move. It moved again. He said to himself, "It is far too small for a man, it is a . . ."

Something hit Mike hard on the back of the head. He fell slightly to one side and rolled down the bank to the stream. When they came to look for him a few minutes later they found him lying with a badly cut head among the yellow blood-drop-emlets that had colonised the stream. In fact the emlets made it look as if he had lost more blood than he had. The police and an ambulance were called and Mike was rushed to the Sussex County Hospital. In the darkness no-one noticed Chelsea-Ann bend down and pick up a large piece of the broken vase. Her curiosity focused not at the outside but the inside as she ran a finger down the cracked porcelain and then gingerly tasted the powder on her finger with the tip of her tongue.

Chapter 5

"Hello.... Hello?... sorry I heard a click and thought we'd been cut off.... I'm fine.... Apparently the head always bleeds a lot.... No, it's quite solid I promise you.... Look, I don't have a car, I wondered if you could pick me up?... Eleven?... Reception.... That's right, the bottom of the tower... Bristol Gate, just around the corner from Eastern Road.... Yes, see you then, Bye."

Mike had woken at first light, when the County Hospital had started to bustle back into life at the beginning of another day. He would probably have rephrased that, because he wasn't actually aware of going to sleep. The unfamiliar sounds, the airlessness, the night staff talking in loud whispers, the ever changing pattern of car headlights on the ceiling, meant he had spent most of the night dozing fitfully.

A young houseman on his rounds had declared him fit enough to go home. The doctor, who hardly looked old enough to be qualified, asked how he planned to get back to Kings Nympton. He suggested that it would be advisable to be driven after a night in hospital. He asked if there was a relative or friend who could come to the rescue? If not, he added, the hospital could call a taxi.

Mike phoned Anna, shaved, bathed and discovered

that whoever had brought his washing things had the foresight to add a clean shirt and a sweater.

By the time Anna drove up the slope to Casualty, Mike was waiting outside in the thin sunlight of an overcast morning. He threw his overnight bag onto the rear seat of the car before climbing in beside her.

"This is very kind."

"I'm glad you're all right. You looked a mess last night. Did you *really* see a dwarf?"

"I'm not sure. Looking back, it's like a bad dream. But I am more determined than ever to find Mervyn and to get to the bottom of whatever's happening in Kings Nympton. That's why I phoned. I thought we could start looking straightaway without wasting any more time."

"Can you manage it?"

"Of course. They only kept me in for observation. I don't even have a plaster on my head. Just a bump above the ear. The only evidence of hospital is an identity bracelet." Mike held his left arm aloft so that his shirt sleeve dropped back to reveal an opaque band of plastic.

"Where do we begin?"

"While I was waiting, I tried to remember any contact that Mervyn had with the antique trade in Brighton. I think there's a dealer in the very small lanes just off Brighton Square."

"Do you remember the name?"

"I don't recall very much. I seem to recollect bumping into Mervyn, a couple of years ago near a shop where he said he always sold Victorian stuff."

They drove into town and parked in West Street and entered the Lanes from Ship Street passing between two second-hand jewellers and an old flint cobbled church. At this point the Lanes became very narrow and resembled a rabbit warren of tiny passages. Mike came to a halt outside a shop called *JUNK AND DIS-ORDERLY*.

"Here we are. I'm *sure* this is it."

It was a small shop fronting onto an alleyway hardly wide enough for two people to pass. In gold lettering on the door it said *Specialists in Victoriana*. The window was full of items from the turn of the century. The limited space was cluttered with Staffordshire Pottery, tins and packages, glass rolling pins, and other household byegones and ephemera. There was a jumble of horse brasses, curios and exotica of every kind.

The shop door bell pinged sharply as they entered. The interior was furnished like a tiny bijou cottage. The three inner walls had been fitted with display shelves from floor to ceiling and were packed with items for sale.

The proprietor was a tall, slightly overweight, American with a dark and even tan that must have come out of a bottle. It certainly hadn't come from the fragile sun of an English spring. His hair was meticulously dressed and streaked. He wore a Cashmere jacket in Burberry's distinctive check. In his hand he had a blue Nailsea glass rolling pin which he was discussing with a customer. He paused and turned to Mike and Anna as they entered. "Do look around, or take a pew. Shan't keep you a moment." He smiled and waved in the direction of two low Victorian nursing chairs.

The reluctant purchaser said, "Do you have one that is not broken."

"Oh, it's meant to be like that," said the American. "All glass rolling pins were individually blown, then snapped off at the end to be filled with tea or spices, corked and given to a sweetheart as a lovegift. If you find one without an end that can be corked, it isn't genuine."

"I'll think about it" said the customer in a tone which suggested that he wouldn't give it another thought. The bell rang as he opened the door to leave and then rattled again as he closed it.

"Now, how can I help you?" trilled the American.

"I'm afraid we're not customers," said Anna, "we're looking for Mervyn Lyle and feel you might be able to help?"

"You don't look like the police," he turned away slightly, but continued to study them with a sideways look.

"We're not," said Mike, "I live in Kings Nympton. We want to see if there is anything we can do to help."

"I thought I recognised you. You are Michael Main aren't you? I've been to *The Old Nail Shot* once or twice. Let me introduce myself, I am Arthur Orage." He pronounced his last name as if it were French. "Last night I decided that if the police called I would tell them everything I know, so I might as well tell you. I simply don't believe what the TV and newspapers are saying. I'm sure Mervyn didn't shoot Malcolm."

"We don't think so either." said Anna.

"That is why we're looking for him. We want to help." The look on Mike's face showed how unsuccessful they had been so far.

The American seemed relieved at an opportunity to talk. "Well, Mervyn came here at lunchtime two days ago, saying that he was in a bit of trouble. He wanted to borrow £200." In this business we help our friends when cash is short.

"Wait a moment," said Anna.

"What time was that?" said Mike simultaneously.

"About 2.30."

"If that is right it means that Mervyn couldn't have been involved in Malcolm's death because we found him at 2.30 just after he had been shot." Then Mike added more slowly, "are you sure about the time?"

"Oh absolutely. I don't close for lunch in the summer, I have a friend who comes in to give me a break at about 2.45. He works in the pub just around the corner and comes in during his lunchtime which he takes at 2.30."

"Did Mervyn say anything else?"

"He said he needed air tickets."

"Air tickets?"

"Yes, I stopped him telling me more and just gave him the money. He's such a nice guy and I've always found him trustworthy. I'd have given him more if he'd asked. He said he would be back in a few days and would settle up. He left as soon as I gave him the money."

"Is that all?"

"Yes."

"Are you sure?"

"Well I think he said something about going to see the landlord of the *Snooty Fox* at Wilmington. But I can't be sure. He said it after he opened the door and there was quite a bit of noise outside."

Mike Main thought for a moment and then said, "This might seem a strange question, do you know if Mervyn had any dealings with a typing agency?"

"Typing?"

"That's right."

"That doesn't sound like Mervyn to me. Antiques, women, wine bars, all that fits with his character, but not typing. Our trade isn't notorious for keeping books and we certainly don't spend much time writing." As an afterthought he added, "An auctioneer maybe, but not an antique dealer – not Mervyn Lyle – and not typing!"

During their conversation, Anna had noticed a bowl

filled with fragile sprays of glass daisies. "Aren't they pretty."

"They're from Portugal. They still make them."

The American handed Anna a bunch for her to look at.

"They *are* lovely, but they must be very difficult to clean?"

"You just wiggle them in sudsie water and give them a blow with your hairdryer."

They laughed because this was obviously something he had said before.

"All right, I'll take three bunches."

The American wrapped them carefully handing them to Anna in a *JUNK AND DISORDERLY* bag.

"Well, Mr Orage, you have been helpful. We will try the *Snooty Fox*. Thank you very much." With that Mike and Anna left, made their way back to the car and took the Lewes road out of Brighton.

From the air, the South Downs look like an enormous barrier built by prehistoric man to hold the sea back. They stretch eighty miles from Hampshire to the great bluff of Beachy Head. The village of Wilmington lies on their northern side, astride the A27, not far from Eastbourne.

Much of the Downs are huge blocks of chalk detached at the beginning of time by long-forgotten rivers which breached the main line of hills. The most easterly massif of chalk, some four miles square, now forms Windover Hill. It rises to over seven hundred feet above the village. Carved on this hillside, is the huge *Long Man of Wilmington*, the tallest hill figure in England. With staves in his outstretched hands he looks as though he is standing guard over the Downs.

Over the years he has been called *Long Man, Lanky Man* and even *Green Man*, when his clean white outline has become overgrown. If paced, his elongated

form measures over 230 feet. The length compensates
for the fore-shortening effect of the sloping hill when
he is viewed from the road. He was probably made by
the Beaker People as long ago as the second millenium
B.C. The Chieftain of such a Neolithic tribe lies buried
on the brow of Windover. At various times he has been
thought to represent St Paul, Mahomet and even the
Indian Hindu deity, Varuna.

The villagers pay very little attention to him,
although they are grateful that he is more modestly
portrayed than the Cerne Abbas figure. If the locals
think about him at all it is as a guide to the weather.
For centuries the people of the Cuckmere Valley have
looked in his direction and said:

> When Firle or Long Man wears a cap
> Then we in the valley will get a drap

Which being translated means, that if either Firle or
Long Man found themselves in the clouds, then rain
was certain. But the thin sunshine persisted as Mike
and Anna took the bypass around Lewes and just
before the Long Man came into view they saw the
Snooty Fox. Anna turned into the car park and found
a space not far from the main entrance.

Once inside the *Snooty Fox*, it was obvious that its
main customers were locals rather than passing trade.
To step over the threshold was to enter a world that
had long ceased to exist in most parts of the British
Isles. The *Foxy Snoot*, as the regulars insisted on calling it, was obviously one of the main watering places
for young fogies in Sussex. They filled the bar in ani-
mated groups, looking as though they were dressed
and ready for a re-make of *Brideshead Revisited*.

The pub was furnished in dark wood and deep red
upholstery. The long bar, affectionately known as
Twickers because of a 1907 photograph of the village
XV on the wall, bristled with genuine hand pumps

for drawing beer up from the cellars. There was no suggestion that it had been chilled. Indeed the beer was as all Englishmen prefer it; slightly to the right of room temperature; no more and no less.

As Mike and Anna entered, a young man in a Leander pink blazer was making his way from the bar with two fists full of foaming tankards. Mike replaced him at the bar. The barman watched the six pints manoeuvre their way into a corner full of rowing hearties, who on receiving refreshment, burst into a stanza of *Green Grow the Rushes O*.

The Barman turned to Mike, "Now, sir, what will it be?"

"Two halves of Theakstons Old Peculiar please."

"Straight or Jug?"

". . . er jug please." Now it was Mike's turn to carry two foaming glasses as he made his way to where Anna had found a seat.

"I hope you don't mind beer. When I got to the bar I discovered the *Snooty Fox* is one of those pubs with a thing about real ale and I didn't have the courage to ask for a gin and tonic or a glass of wine. Silly really . . . because by no means everybody is drinking beer."

"It's just right," said Anna with a laugh. "It's not my usual drink, but I am thirsty, so what could be better."

As they enjoyed their drink they planned the next move which would be to speak to the publican and see if he knew anything about Mervyn. They dearly hoped to discover a reason for Mervyn's connection with a typing agency, or at least a clue about the drawings by Eric Gill.

"I suppose we might as well get on with what we've come to do." Mike braced himself for the task. As he stood he picked up the empty glasses. "I'll speak to the barman. Would you like another?"

"No thank you."

"It doesn't have to be beer."

"No, that was really enough for me."

Mike arrived back at the bar during a lull in business. The thirst of the young fogies had been temporarily assuaged or perhaps they were making their drinks last a little longer.

"Would you put another half in there please?"

"Certainly. Old Particular?"

"No, Peculiar."

"Of course." The barman pulled a generous measure into his glass. "There we are, that'll be 65 pence please."

"Would it be possible to speak to the landlord? I'm afraid I don't know his name."

"Something wrong?"

"No, I'm making enquiries about a mutual friend."

"Oh I see, he's in the other bar. It's Mr Haslam sir, Derek Haslam. I'll get him to come to you. You're over there with the lady by the window?"

"That's right."

Mike made his way back to Anna. He was about to explain his conversation with the barman when a pleasant looking man in his mid forties came through the door from the adjoining bar. He put his drink down on the table next to Mike's glass and sat down at one of the empty chairs. He smiled. "Hello I'm Derek Haslam. Fred tells me you would like a word."

"Yes. We're trying to find Mervyn Lyle and wondered if you could help?"

"You should talk to the police. They're looking for him too."

"I live in Kings Nympton. Mervyn is obviously in trouble, we want to help if we can."

"Well I'm afraid I don't know where he is."

"Do you know if he has any connection with a typing agency?"

"Typing? Mervyn Lyle? I shouldn't think so."

"Well what about drawings by Eric Gill?"

". . . er I'm not interested in anything like that."

"Like what?"

"Shall we say . . . naughty pictures?"

"I didn't say anything about naughty pictures."

"True, but you did say Eric Gill and there is a local market for a certain sort of art . . . pictures by Eric Gill, Aubrey Beardsley and bronzes by a Frenchman called Rodin."

Anna had been silent during the conversation. She had been deep in thought resting an index finger on her lips. She moved her hand. "Anyone can look at pictures by Eric Gill or Aubrey Beardsley. The British Museum has a whole portfolio so does the Victoria and Albert and the University of Texas. Anyone can ask to see them. But if I want to buy one" she paused "where would I go?"

Derek Haslam didn't look quite so relaxed. He finished his drink. "That is . . . er not information that is generally made public."

Mike spoke firmly. "Look we're talking about a shooting. Someone has been killed. Mervyn is a friend. The police are involved. We want to do something to help. If you can tell us where we could get drawings by Eric Gill like the ones you have mentioned, that may give us a lead to Mervyn's whereabouts."

Derek Haslam relaxed. "There's little art gallery on the Plumpton Green road to Ditchling. It's run by a man called McBride. . . . Harry McBride, he's the local supplier."

Having got something substantial at last, Anna wasn't going to be fobbed off with insufficient information. "When we get to the gallery how do we make sure that Mr McBride understands which pictures we are talking about?"

"Say, Derek Haslam sent you. Ask him to phone me
if he needs confirmation."

"Thank you."

"My pleasure." Derek Haslam rose and started to
make his way back to the other bar. The look on his
face suggested very little pleasure, if any at all.

When he had gone, Mike turned to Anna, "I think
we have got our *first* real clue."

"To Ditchling," was her response.

They started to leave. At that moment they spotted
Mr and Mrs Wayne Lane sitting in the corner of the
bar. They waved to them as they left. Wayne Lane
responded with a very weak smile and the most half-
hearted of waves.

Fifty miles away, in the City of London, two young
Insurance brokers from Kings Nympton sat down for
lunch in *The Captain's Room*, the restaurant below
the futuristic Lloyd's building. They spent the meal
deep in conversation. When the coffee arrived, they
pushed their chairs back, to give themselves greater
freedom. "I think we were wise to spend the last hour
planning our strategy for the next few months," said
one.

The other took a deep breath, "I agree. The girls are
so much better at it than we are."

"Well – They have more time."

"That, sounds very nearly, a sexist remark to me."

"I mean – They're at home while we have to work."

"Careful."

"You know very well what I'm trying to say –
They're at home and we're here."

"Of course."

"They certainly did well with Claire from the restaurant."

"Mmm. And now Mike is our job."

"We're getting there, and with the vicar too."

The Dragon's Back

"Let's go for a series of dinner parties if we can get the right speakers. Do you think Dick will do one?"

"It would be marvellous if he would."

"We'd better get back to work and earn a crust or two."

They both laughed, rose from their table, settled their bills and returned to their offices.

Chapter 6

Ditchling is a quiet little Sussex village north of the Downs about six miles from Brighton. It is difficult to imagine, but in Saxon times *Diccelingas* was the thrusting administrative centre of a royal estate. The evidence of pre-Conquest times abound in the church and in the churchyard and it is not too difficult to find the influence of Eric Gill on recent headstones. The girdle of houses edging the High Street is a haphazard assortment of small half-timbered dwellings standing side-by-side with Georgian elegance, while in the side streets the buildings lean across the road towards each other, like elderly people trying to follow the drift of a conversation.

There was no chance that Mike and Anna would miss the gallery as they drove in along the main road from Plumpton Green. A large free-standing bronze stood in the centre of the ample grass that ran down to the road. It was a towering figure of Honoré de Balzac in a Churchillian pose. His hands were thrust down deep into his pockets, while his coat reached the ground and was swept back, giving the impression that he was bracing himself against a storm from the sea. His eyes were fixed on the Downs almost as if he was trying to look through them to his native land to see how it was faring in the gale.

A discreet sign to the gallery pointed down the drive that wound its way past the farmhouse. Originally the car park, now tarmacked, would have been the farmyard. The restored outhouses, barn and main buildings surrounded three sides of the car park. The barn had two dutch gables and parked immediately below one, was a red van. What must have been a hoist for lifting heavy sacks of grain was now being used to manoeuvre a bronze figure into the van.

Anna parked near the open side of the car park and momentarily glanced at a pleasant view through a handful of beech trees to the open countryside and Offham Hill in the distance.

As one young man in overalls stowed the hoisting gear through an opening in the gable, another secured the bronze in the van. A tall, fairly distinguished middle aged man approached Mike and Anna.

"Can I help?" He spoke with a gentle Highland brogue.

"We are looking for Mr McBride."

"That's me. If you'll let me get the delivery details for the driver, I'll be with you. Have a browse in the Gallery." He waved in the direction of the door, "Paintings on the left, bronzes on the right and prints upstairs."

Stepping inside, they entered a building that had been perfectly adapted to create a gallery. In reality little had been done. The cob walls had been whitened and the beams, already ancient timber when they had been incorporated into the building, remained their rich dark mellow brown. Apart from the lighting track for movable spot lights and a sanded wooden floor, the building was as it had always been. Yet somehow it had become a natural setting for works of art. The paintings to the left were all huge canvasses of Brighton with the unmistakable touch of Philip Dunn. They captured the hot sun over a bandstand; a girl in a

Hockneyesque swimming pool; geometrically striped deck chairs whose occupants were seen as shadows cast by the sun as it sank into a vivid blue acrylic sea. All very much the establishment of contemporary art in Brighton. By contrast, at the other end of the gallery was a collection of bronzes that appeared to be by Augustus Rodin. If they weren't his, they were definitely European and most probably French.

Mike and Anna hadn't really had time to look at either the paintings or the bronzes and were in the process of moving from the works of Philip Dunn to the other end of the gallery when Harry McBride reappeared.

"Now what can I show you?"

"Are these *really* by Rodin?" Anna was a little hesitant because although her heart said they were, her mind said there couldn't possibly be so many genuine Rodins for sale in one small Sussex gallery.

"No, actually they're not, but aren't they good? The artist is a local man who wants to keep the creative spirit alive in Ditchling. We sell quite a number because they are so good. He seems to have caught the virile strength and movement of Rodin. Is there one that interests you?" He turned to Mike, "What can I show you?"

"Actually" Mike paused. He wasn't quite sure how to ask for erotic pictures in what, by all appearance, was a respectable gallery. Not that he would have found it easier in one that wasn't. In the end he said rather lamely, "It's er . . . prints we're after."

"They're upstairs" Harry McBride led the way, "We've just had in a new series by John Piper and I've managed to find a few old Lowries."

Anna was beginning to realise that she would have to take the lead in the conversation. "I think we must be perfectly honest," she said, "We're trying to find the source of some drawings by Eric Gill. Not the sort that normally come onto the market. Derek Haslam sent us. He said if we mentioned his name you would understand what we are looking for." By the time Anna had reached the top step she felt a little uncomfortable but it wasn't as a result of climbing the stairs.

"It isn't normally the ladies who want to see them" Harry McBride was a little surprised.

Anna felt she had to explain, "We are looking for someone called Mervyn Lyle. We want to help him. And somehow we think there's a connection between him and the drawings."

"You are right of course" Harry McBride had taken a large red portfolio from a storage rack and laid it on one side of the table. He untied the strings so that he could display the drawings for Mike and Anna. "Are you sure that you want to see these?"

"No I don't think we need to, I teach the history of art and have made a special study of Eric Gill so I know the sort of drawings he occasionally did. Are they original? I saw some recently which weren't genuine."

"Right again, it is the same man who does the Rodins. His work is excellent but he doesn't want his name known. He's a Frenchman. Mervyn Lyle came to me about two years ago with a list of the things he wanted, mainly copies of erotic bronzes by Rodin and some drawings by Gill and Beardsley."

"Do go on."

"Now he takes a regular supply. I don't know where they go. He was due to take some this week. He came in a couple of days ago and said I would have to keep them for a little longer. When I saw the TV news later . . . about the shooting in Kings Nympton . . . I presumed that was the reason for the delay. He said he was going away for a few days."

"We don't think he did the shooting" said Anna firmly.

"It didn't sound like Mervyn Lyle to me."

"Did he say where he was going?" enquired Mike.

"Guernsey."

"Are you sure?"

"Yes St Peter Port. A boat in the harbour."

"Did he give its name?"

"No, he just said a frigate in St Peter Port."

"Well that's a help. Thank you." Anna looked relieved that they were getting somewhere at last.

As they made their way back down the stairs, Mike turned and said, "With your help, I think we might be nearer to finding Mervyn. Thank you."

They shook hands at the door.

"I'm sorry I haven't been able to sell you anything," said Harry McBride with a smile, "but if there is anything I can do to help Mervyn, let me know."

As Anna led the way back to the car she turned and said over her shoulder, "I think you've interested us in quite a lot, I'll certainly be back to look at the Lowries and I would like to see an Eric Gill if you could find a genuine one."

They were soon heading back to Kings Nympton which was just over the A27 from Ditchling.

When they arrived Anna, parked in front of Mike's cottage, "What next?"

"I think we must go to Guernsey. St Peter Port is a very small place, if Mervyn is hiding there it shouldn't be too difficult to find him. I'll book seats on a plane for tomorrow. I'll phone you with the time of the flight. We could meet at Gatwick. Bring an overnight bag, just in case."

Anna shook her head slowly and sighed "I don't think we're any nearer to solving the problem, we already knew there was a link between Mervyn and the drawings."

"True. But Harry McBride is another link. And we now know where Mervyn is hiding." Mike hesitated before he added, "I'm fascinated by the whole idea of erotic pictures. The drawings that the Major showed you at the Manor, were they . . . ?"

"No they were superb pen and ink sketches of a model. Eric Gill illustrated the Song of Solomon and Major Bradford had some of the bride preparing for her husband. They were beautiful – but wouldn't be classed as erotic and they weren't by Eric Gill."

"I suppose if I'd stopped to think about it, I would have realised that artists must do such work. But you spoke as if there was a lot of pictures. Even collections in some places."

"It depends on the artist. Both Eric Gill and Auguste Rodin were sculptors with a great interest in the human body. I don't think their interest was necessarily prurient. Their drawings were often attempts to see how the body worked or simply celebrations of beauty. Rodin had a dark and morbid side and Mary McArthur's recent biography of Eric Gill has revealed he was a little odd. Yes, there are large collections by both men that aren't put on show, but they're available for anyone doing research."

"Well" said Mike Main, "you learn something new every day." He opened the car door and started to get out.

The stillness of the village was suddenly shattered as a powerful motor cycle exploded into the road from Kissing Tree Lane. Mike straightened up to see who had violated the peace with such an awful noise. As the rider flashed by Mike saw it was a policeman, carapaced and goggled. If he hadn't looked up at that moment he wouldn't have noticed the car about fifty yards behind. It appeared to have Wayne Lane at the wheel with his wife next to him. Mike bent down and spoke into the car, "Did you see who that was?"

"The motor cyclist?"

"No, in the car."

"Who?"

"The taxi driver from New York."

"Is that important?"

"I don't know. But the fact that they were also at Wilmington is too much of a coincidence." He sighed, "you *are* right. We're not any closer to discovering what's happening. Why not come in and have a coffee so that we can make plans for tomorrow?"

A few moments later they were seated in the kitchen. After the coffee had been made Mike said, "Apart from the link with Harry McBride, the loan from the American antique dealer and the fact that we now know where Mervyn is hiding, we are no further forward." Mike clenched his fist and gently pounded the kitchen table. "We still need to find out if Mervyn really did the shooting? If he didn't, who did? And most importantly, we must discover what Malcolm was trying to say."

"So a fresh start tomorrow in Guernsey?" Anna smiled.

Mike nodded, there was nothing that they could do now so he idly turned over a small pile of mail that had been left on the kitchen table. It consisted mostly of leaflets and brochures advertising free offers with one or two other items that had been pushed through the letterbox, including *The Parish Magazine of St Rumons*.

"I think I've got it," said Anna with a cry of delight, closing her eyes and gently hitting her brow with the palm of her hand.

"You know who did the shooting?"

"No, . . . the vicar."

"I don't see . . ."

"When we were introduced to him at the Manor, he said his previous job had been in the North, then later at the vicarage, he told us his hobby was the flora of Sussex. He certainly knows a lot about the flowers of this area and local history. That doesn't make sense if he's been living and working in the North."

"Mmm . . ."

"I've had a nagging feeling since we met him that something didn't ring true. But I couldn't put my finger on it." Anna looked directly at Mike, "now we *know* he is hiding something."

"Yes, but what?"

"I wish I knew." She smoothed the sleeve of her blouse. "And then there's the Chinese vase. That's another lead we haven't unravelled."

"And the clue about the typing agency."

"We haven't made any real progress, have we?"

At the same moment, they both reached to pick up the parish magazine, and their fingers touched. Mike deliberately took hold of Anna's hand and looked as though he was about to say something, but he stopped, and let go of her hand. During those few brief seconds the feeling had been mutual and it spoke volumes when words would have been inadequate. Mike pushed back his chair and stood, breaking the silence.

"A fresh start tomorrow. I'll phone Gilbertravel and get the tickets. It would be silly to take two cars to Gatwick so I'll pick you up. I'll let you know the time of the flight."

Not long afterwards Anna was making the now familiar journey up Kissing Tree Lane and over the Downs to Brighton. It was too early in the evening for badgers, but they were very much in her mind.

Chapter 7

"The flight shouldn't last more than an hour." Mike spoke as he changed gear to leave the M23 on the spur road to Gatwick. "My business friends tell me, that if we use Level 1 in Car Park 2 we can walk straight into departures. Let's see if they are right." They sped past the Hilton and were soon climbing the spiral ramp into the Short Term Car Park and found an empty space on the appropriate floor.

A few moments later they checked-in at the *GUERNSEY ISLAND AIRWAYS* desk in the main concourse. A uniformed young woman looked up and smiled as she took their tickets. "How are you today?"

"Fine."

"Smoking or non-smoking?"

"Non-smoking please."

"Do you have any luggage?"

"Two overnight bags." Mike held them up and put them on the counter so that hand-luggage labels could be attached to each piece.

"Thank you."

"You're welcome. Here are your boarding cards. You're seated in row 4 in the non-smoking section and should be boarding in about twenty minutes time through Gate One. You will find that . . ." She stood and lent over the counter to point the way "down the steps and through Domestic Departures."

"Thank you."

"Have a good flight."

They spent a few moments in the *Sky Shop* buying newspapers and magazines and had hardly arrived at the Gate before a tannoy announced, "Good Morning Ladies and Gentlemen. We need to bus you to your plane today. Please make sure that you have all your belongings with you. And would you extinguish all cigarettes and refrain from smoking until you have boarded your aircraft and the no-smoking signs have been switched off."

The air was heavy with aviation fuel as they drove past orderly ranks of airliners in familiar liveries. Most seemed to tower above the bus but the further they drove, the smaller they became. When the bus finally came to a halt near a perimeter fence, there was a murmur of disapproval from the other passengers when they caught sight of their aircraft.

"Is that really our plane?" Anna turned to Mike with a hint of apprehension. "Do we really have to travel in that? It looks like a *Deux Chevaux* with wings."

A group of elderly passengers struggled from the bus, still voicing their unhappiness at the airline's choice of aircraft. The men were being blasé about the big jets that had carried them on previous holidays. The same tour operator's labels on each piece of their hand luggage marked them off as a party bound for the same hotel.

As Mike and Anna stood in an untidy queue waiting to board, Mike said "In spite of everyone's displeasure, our plane is one of the successes of British industry. It is a *Short Three-Sixty* and is ideal for an island like Guernsey. One of my regulars at *The Old Nail Shot* sells them. The Americans love their quietness and use them on the feeder routes into their big cities."

Once on board they were quickly airborne and heading South-West over the Channel with Portsmouth visible below their port wing. Anna said "I don't know much about boats. When we find the harbour, how do we recognise a frigate? And if we find one, how do we know it is the one we are looking for?"

"I did a little research last night." Mike fished a piece of paper from the inside pocket of his jacket and found the travel agent's itinerary which was blank on one side. Using a magazine as a pad, he drew a rough boat shape. "My dictionary told me that a frigate was a square rigged vessel of the eighteenth or nineteenth century, or it's a fast naval craft, smaller than a destroyer. Whenever I have been to St Peter Port the harbour has been full of pleasure crafts; dinghies, yachts, cabin cruisers and a handful of fishing boats. I don't remember seeing a square rigged boat and I am not expecting more than one today. If there are several, we will just have to wait until we spot Mervyn." Mervyn's name was now added to the notes. "I doubt if he would be involved with a naval vessel, but if there is a modern frigate in the harbour, we'll take a look at that too."

"What do we do when we find him?"

"Ask what happened."

"Why he shot Malcolm, if he did."

"Yes and if the explanation is reasonable, try to get him to go back to Brighton to sort it out with the police."

"Is that the best way to help?"

"It's the only way. The shooting was out of character. There must be an explanation. We could arrange for a good lawyer . . ."

"But it's not as simple as that." Anna broke into what Mike was saying. "There was also a burglary, a vicar who was not telling the truth, forged drawings and some questionable art, you were hit over the head twice, . . . oh, and the dwarfs."

"I had forgotten about them." Mike placed the fingers of one hand on his brow and with the other doodled more hieroglyphics on the piece of paper. He turned to Anna and sighed "What do you suggest?"

"Find Mervyn first and hear what he has to say."

"Mmm . . ."

They drifted into silence thinking about the events of the last few days. The steady, rhythm of the engines had a soporific effect. A stewardess put a tray of sandwiches in front of them, their neatly cut triangles lying on a bed of fresh lettuce.

"That reminds me" said Anna "did you finish your article?"

"Yes and made notes for the next."

"Oh what will it be about?"

"Leeks."

"You're teasing?"

"No, I'll deal with how they've left their mark on England."

"Shouldn't that be Wales?"

"No, they go back to ancient Egypt and gradually spread into Europe. The Irish, Danes and the English used them long before the Welsh."

"Being the emblem of Wales, I presumed that was where they came from. How did they come to be associated with the Welsh?"

"I haven't found a satisfactory answer to that, only legends and they aren't very convincing. I suspect that it was because they grow easily in a poor wet soil and the Welsh grew to depend on them, using them long after they had ceased to be fashionable in England."

"Why do you say that?"

"A man called John Parkinson, a sixteenth century herbalist says they were food for the poor in England, while in Wales, they were 'the general feeding of the vulgar gentleman'. Vulgar meaning 'ordinary' I think."

"What about recipes?"

"There aren't many because in England we stopped using them for nearly three hundred years."

"Mrs Beeton?"

"Not very inspiring on the subject."

"What will you do?"

"Oh that's easy. I will write about the two great soups created by Louis Diat in New York fifty years ago. He invented *Vichyssoise* using one of his mother's recipes and named it after her home town. And the other will be the hot version – the *Bonne Femme*."

"Mmmm, I love Vichyssoise."

At that moment the engine noise changed and the stewardess announced, "Ladies and Gentlemen we are about to land in Guernsey. Please make sure that your seat belts are fastened and that you have returned your seat to the upright position.

Like a speed boat crossing the wash of another vessel, the *Short Three-Sixty* started to chop through the turbulence of a thin layer of cloud. A rocky coast, cultivated fields and acres of greenhouses passed swiftly below them as they made their final approach.

For such a tiny airport the terminal building had a large number of car hire firms offering their services. In addition to the local companies were all the familiar international names. Mike hired a Sierra from the Hertz counter and spent the first mile of the drive into St Peter Port adjusting to the slow pace of the island's traffic.

"I *like* the idea of a thirty-five miles an hour speed limit," said Anna. "I'd love to live here."

"It's certainly undemanding." Mike re-aligned the rear view mirror as he spoke. "But it must get rather tedious if you live here all the time."

"Does everybody keep it?"

"Most roads are rather like this, so don't lend themselves to roaring away at high speed."

"They must save a lot of money on petrol and cars."

"I don't think they save on cars, except through low tax. Cars are a status symbol here as much as anywhere else. The only difference is that even the most powerful have to be driven at thirty-five miles per hour . . . how frustrating that must be."

They turned the corner on the crest of the hill to descend into St Peter Port, a Jaguar XJS passed them going in the opposite direction at a funereal pace.

"I see what you mean."

Having reached sea level, they drove along the front of St Peter Port until they found a parking space on *Glategny Esplanade*, just beyond the ferry quay. They got out into the warm afternoon sunlight.

"I don't think there is a square rigged ship here." Mike spoke across the roof of the Sierra as he withdrew the key from the lock and tugged at the handle to make sure it was shut.

Anna looked up at the terraced buildings of this tiny, French looking fishing port. Granite houses with mellow red roofs rose in tiers from the water's edge. The buildings formed an amphitheatre overlooking the harbour with the grim stronghold of Castle Cornet standing firmly at the end of the long arm of the stone pier. In the distance was the island of Herm and beyond that, Sark.

Having taken in the scene Anna turned to Mike who had his back to the sea. Behind him, across the narrow esplanade was a low sea wall guarding a forest of masts belonging to the vessels in the North Beach Marina. The slackened halliards were striking the metal masts at a furious tempo, reaching crescendos of tintinnabulated sound that rose and fell with the breeze.

"Let's cross here" said Mike "As we are this end of town we might as well look in the new Marina first."

Once across the road they walked to the steps that led down to the landing stage and the individual berths. Vessels of every size and shape filled the available space. Even from the most cursory glance it was obvious that there wasn't a frigate there. Indeed it would have been impossible for a vessel of that size to gain access into the Marina.

They climbed back to the esplanade and walked past the *Careening Hard* towards the town church. On their left were two more small basins for pleasure craft. Again, it was obvious that they didn't contain a frigate. Mike and Anna soon reached Castle Pier which provided a road link with Castle Cornet and the lighthouse. Walking its full length they looked to see if a frigate might have dropped anchor in the deep water beyond the harbour entrance, or in Havelet Bay. But none were to be seen. A ferry hooted twice with a low reverberating shudder, warning small boats in the harbour entrance that it was about to cast off and continue its journey to St Malo. A cluster of sea gulls descended noisily onto some jetsam.

Anna broke the silence as they walked back towards the Bus Terminal end of the pier.

"What do we do now?"

"Get some food, I think that's the first thing. I am not looking after you very well. Apart from the sandwiches on the plane we haven't eaten properly today. Let's have an early supper and decide if we want to catch the last plane or stay the night and continue looking tomorrow."

"That sounds a good idea," said Anna "The ferry almost covered the rumbles in my tummy just now."

"Let's try *Le Nautique*, just up the steps over there" Mike pointed along the quay. "It's a favourite haunt of sailors and has a marvellous view over the harbour."

The evening rush hadn't started so they managed to get a table near the window. It was only after they were seated that Mike remembered Anna wasn't particularly fond of sea food.

"I had forgotten that fish isn't your favourite food. I chose this because the sea food is so good but I am sure you could have whatever you like – please do."

"You mustn't worry. As I said before it's school cooking that has spoiled fish for me. I enjoyed the hot pâté in Brighton so I have already discovered that I enjoy whatever you order. Please choose for both of us."

A waiter appeared and taking their napkins, he unfurled and spread them across their laps. He then gave them a menu adding a wine list for Mike who asked "What's the special on your menu today?"

"I'll get the chef, Sir," the waiter lisped obsequiously.

A few moments later the chef appeared with a wooden platter set with Sea Bream, Sea Bass, Brill, Red Mullet all decorated with ice, lemons, seaweed, spider crabs, and Amandes de Mer.

"The Sea Bream looks very tempting. How do you cook them?"

"A la Vendangeuse, Sir."

"Grape-Pickers?"

"That's right."

"I think we will try that. Sea Bream for two please, and some of your delicious vegetables. We'll begin with the Assiette of Smoked Fish. Do you still serve that, with a little salmon caviar?"

"We do, Sir."

"Excellent and a bottle of Pouilly Fumé."

"Certainly."

The chef hurried away while Mike and Anna looked out of the window. A yacht had come through the entrance of the Victoria Marina under gentle engine power. The crew were stowing the sails and making fast various sheets and lines. One member put fenders out on the starboard side. The helmsman cut the engine and swung her safely into her berth. Another crew member jumped ashore and secured her fore and aft.

Much later as they drank coffee Mike said "Well decision time. Do we catch the last plane or stay and continue looking tomorrow?"

"Stay until tomorrow." For the first time Anna felt relaxed and sure of herself and yet was surprised by the firmness of her decision. So she quickly continued "I would like to see Victor Hugo's house – maybe we could fit that in, if we stayed?"

"I didn't know that he had lived here?" Mike turned and watched another yacht slide into its berth. The light was beginning to fade so the activities of the crew were bathed in the red and green glow of the vessel's navigational lights.

"I was reading a biography recently. I think it said he lived here for several years. His house must have been on one of the terraces much higher up. His work room was built into the roof and it gave him a view of Herm and Sark and enabled him to see France, which inspired him, so he said."

"I know very little about Victor Hugo, but I would like to see his house – you never know the kitchen might be open to the public too."

"You've got a one track mind."

"Nonsense. The great literary figures of France always had an interest in food. André Dumas poured his last energies into his *Grand Dictionnaire de Cuisine*."

They both laughed.

Mike turned to look for a waiter to order more coffee. *Le Nautique* had filled up in the last hour. Most of the diners were dressed in faded sweaters, jeans and espadrilles and had that deep mahogany tan which can only be acquired at sea. The bar area was full of people enjoying a drink while they waited for a table.

There was a strange yet familiar figure on one of the bar stools. He seemed to nod in their direction. The combination of the lighting from the bar which was behind him, and his yachting cap meant that his face was concealed in a shadow. He was wearing sailing clothes in the way a non-swimmer might wear a wetsuit; they didn't look right and he looked uncomfortable. What could be seen of the backs of his hands and his face had the pallor associated with the land not the sea.

Mike caught and returned his stare. The stranger jumped down from his stool and came towards them. "Hello Mr Main."

"Mervyn. What are you doing here?"

"I could ask you the same question."

"Well we are looking for you. Come and sit down." Mike pointed to a vacant chair. At the same moment he managed to catch the attention of the waiter. "More coffee please and could you bring another cup?" He turned back to Mervyn "Do you remember Miss Richardson. I think you met when we had a drink at the Major's?"

Mervyn didn't appear to have heard the question "I am in a bit of trouble, Mr Main."

"That's why we're here. We don't think that you shot Malcolm."

"I didn't." Mervyn sighed deeply. "I've got to wear this get-up because all the papers 'ave 'ad my picture plastered across the front page."

"Who shot Malcolm?" said Anna.

"I don't know."

"Then why are you here?" Anna's question implied a hidden accusation.

Mervyn was silent.

"Mervyn we want to help" pleaded Mike "but we need to know what is going on."

Mervyn was silent again for a few moments but they waited for him to speak. "It goes back about three years, to the time when my sister was at college. She was the bright one of the family. During her final exams someone offered her cocaine. I don't think she really knew what it was. They told her it was what the early morning TV presenters use to concentrate and get by on little sleep. I don't know what happened but it appears that at a celebration party, when she got her degree, she took a little more and then had too much champagne. In the morning she was dead. The verdict was an overdose of drugs and alcohol." Mervyn paused and looked out of the window with unseeing eyes. "It's the pushers who are the killers and whoever they work for. I've been looking for them ever since. Last week Malcolm was offered some information. I came here to look into it." In a disjointed way he added "By what the papers say I was at Gatwick at the time of the shooting. But I can't prove it and I shouldn't think anyone can."

"We heard you were on a boat." Mike rearranged the salt and pepper on the table.

"Not me. The boat was the bit of information that Malcolm got, and I came to follow it up. An old man down by the docks told me the sort of boat I was looking for. It's one of those old ones, like they 'ave in the Tall Ships Race. It 'asn't appeared yet. It was getting dark so I came in for a drink and some grub."

"Will the drugs be on the boat?" asked Anna.

"I don't know. Malcolm met a student in Brighton. I think he had just got the habit in a bad way and he was at the stage when he would sell his grandmother to get money for another fix. Malcolm bought what he was selling; a piece of paper that said 'a frigate in St Peter Port'."

"It doesn't sound very much to me?"

"Well it was enough to get him shot, and the fact that they killed him means it was reliable information. They didn't want it to get any further did they?"

"True."

"It's a funny place St Peter Port." Having spoken about his problems Mervyn appeared to relax and became more expansive. "It must be a thieves paradise. Every other building is a bank. There must be more banks than bars, and that's saying something."

"That doesn't necessarily mean that everyone is a criminal?" said Anna.

"I don't mean criminal in that way. It's a tax fiddle i'nit? All the big businessmen do it. They keep their loot offshore away from the hands of the Inland Revenue. The small businessmen here, making their money from the hire-car racket."

Mike had stopped playing with the salt and pepper and had now put a spare knife and fork "in formation astern"; like two ships following one behind the other along the table. "How does that work? We hired a brand new Sierra this morning at an absurd price."

"They come from the Continent and spend a few weeks here as hire cars. Then they go to England and sell as very low mileage cars and escape the tax you normally have to pay on foreign cars."

"I couldn't work out why . . ."

"Come on" said Anna briskly "We still have a lot to discuss." Turning to Mervyn she said "What is the connection between your sister's death and the er . . . the pictures you got from Ditchling?"

"How did you find out about them?"

"Mervyn we have been looking everywhere" said Mike with a certain amount of exasperation. "An American in *Junk and Disorderly* told us to go to the *Snooty Fox* at Wilmington and from there we found

out about Harry McBride. Incidentally you told me
that you didn't deal in pictures."

"Well I don't really, it's a side-line. It's hardly legit-
imate art, is it? It's not the sort of thing I want people
to know about in Kings Nympton."

"Even the Major now says he didn't get any pictures
from you."

"That's true. I got those Eric Gills for him to look
at. But in the end he didn't want them, so I took them
back."

"Are the pictures connected with your sister's
death?" questioned Anna.

"No way."

"And what about the dwarfs and the funny American couple." Anna continued the list of clues.

"Everybody's talking about the dwarfs but I haven't
seen them. What do the Americans look like? Is he a
big Italian looking fellow with not much hair?"

"That's right. He is a taxi driver from New York.
She's quite small and dark. He always wears a blazer
and she prefers denim."

"He's not a taxi driver. Police more like it. They
were down at the new Marina this afternoon looking
over the boats. I followed them back to a hotel and
managed to get a look at the book they signed at
reception. They booked into two single rooms. He
signed the books as 'Lane' and she signed it as 'Ferrari'. I remember thinking, she's a pretty fast one,
but obviously not fast enough to be sharing the same
room."

"Do you *know* they are police?"

"Well I haven't seen it written down. They look like
it. You can spot them a mile away."

Mervyn unsuccessfully stifled a yawn.

"You're tired."

"I've been up since first light for the last two days."

"What should we do?" said Anna.

"Meet tomorrow and give the frigate one more day," suggested Mike.

"O.K." said Mervyn "I might get up early, so why don't we meet at the Ferry Terminal at 9.30? I'm booked into a hotel on the sea front."

"Where is the best place for us to stay?" Mike had finally abandoned the things he had been playing with on the table.

"There is a big hotel on the top of the hill called the O.G.H., *Old Government House*. It's a palm court sort of place."

"I think we want something smaller and quieter." Mike caught the attention of the waiter.

"More coffee, Sir?"

"No thank you. We need a bit of information. We want a nice quiet hotel: a comfortable place. Where would you suggest?"

"For you and the lady, sir? Oh, that's easy. La Frégate."

"Would you say that again, *slowly*" said Mike, thinking that he might have misheard.

"It is up the hill, Sir. *La Frégate*. The Frigate."

Chapter 8

La Frégate was really a restaurant with rooms. The dining room had a spectacular view over the harbour and the old town. In the distance the Cherbourg Peninsular created a firm line between the blurred blue of the sea and sky. Immediately above the restaurant was a single corridor of rooms that shared the same view. Most hotels list the services their guests can expect, La Frégate simply announced "No animals, no children, no radio and no television." But far from making a cold and cheerless atmosphere, the *Toffanello* family had created a small comfortable home from home for the traveller.

Mike and Anna had approached the hotel along Vauxlaurels Lane, one a series of tiny alleyways, that terraced the hillside upon which much of St Peter Port was perilously perched.

After a night's rest Mike had joined Anna on the balcony of her room for breakfast. Enjoying the warm sunshine, the fresh scent of a summer morning, the chatter of hopeful sparrows, the aromatic and musk smells wafting from the herbs and lilies in the gardens below and, perhaps above all, reluctant to break the spell that they were finding in each other's company, they sat for longer than they had intended. This meant that just before 9.30 they had to hurry down the slippery cobblestones of Beauregard Lane to the Ferry Terminal. It had been immediately below them during breakfast, when it appeared a toylike scene peopled with minute figures and miniature cars and lorries. Now, as they approached it, it had all the noise, dust and smell of a busy port. Last minute travellers hurried to secure a place on the ferry before the gaping mouth of its bow doors were winched shut.

"Did you sleep well?" Mike greeted Mervyn when they met on the Esplanade.

"Like a top. It did me the world of good just being able to talk last night."

"Any idea what we should do?"

"I think." Mervyn paused as a car overladen with returning holiday makers, pushed its way onto the quay hoping to catch the Weymouth ferry. "Malcolm's information obviously referred to someone who has already stayed at The Frigate." He made no attempt to pronounce the name in French. "We could go back there and try to find out who it was. I expect the clues will have gone cold by now, but we could try. Then we might as well as go back to Kings Nympton. There is no point in staying here." As an afterthought he added ruefully, "I suppose I will have to give myself up?"

"We'll come with you" insisted Anna. "They must see that you couldn't possibly have shot Malcolm. The American from *Junk and Disorderly* said he would confirm that you were with him at 2.30. He promised us that."

"All right." Mike spoke decisively making up his mind for all of them. "Let's go back to La Frégate and see if we can find out, who it was, who stayed there. By the time we get there, we will need a cup of coffee to revive us."

The sun which had felt gently warm at breakfast was already reflecting a shimmering heat from the roads and pavements at sea level.

Mervyn wiped his brow with a single movement of a hand. "It's going to be hot."

"Even on a frosty morning, I imagine it would warm the coldest blood to walk up to La Frégate."

At this stage Anna had missed the talk about the day's temperature and was looking up at the name of a side road. "We spent so much time yesterday looking at boats that I hadn't realised that Guernsey was so French. Look at the name over there." she pointed, "And the names of those companies in that building." In the doorway opposite were several brass plates. They declared, *Michelle Bounichou Jardin Meubles, Grand Vins de Perigord and Pierre de Malville, Lawyer.*

"Come on let's begin" Mike urged them to make a start up the zig-zag path that led to La Frégate. He was already slightly out of breath when he said "Last night we forgot . . . to ask you about . . . typing services."

"You what?"

"Typing agencies."

"What d'you mean?"

"Well the last thing Malcolm said was something about 'Typing Services'. Does that mean anything?"

"Nothing." Then it struck Mervyn what Mike was saying. "D'mean you spoke to him after he was shot?"

"Yes."

"Howja do that?"

"We were looking for you" said Anna.

"Your front door was locked so we went around to the side door and heard the knocking and found Malcolm. He died just after saying 'typing services'."

"Must've been awful."

"It was. I will never be able to get it out of my mind." said Anna.

"And the vases?"

"Vases?"

"The K'ang Hsi vases. When we arrived they were in your side window."

"Those."

"Where did you get them."

"Hallelujah Harry."

"Are you sure?"

"Yes. Why?"

"The vicar thinks that you gave one to Harry for helping with a heavy load."

"It's true Harry helps me occasionally but the vases came from him. He discovered them somewhere. He won't say where exactly, he's shy about it. They're not the real thing, but they're very good copies."

"And when we got outside, after Malcolm had died, they were gone." Mike continued.

"Gone? Someone pinched them and left the other things? . . . even the chair in the window is Charles II. They don't know much about antiques that's all I can say."

By now, they had reached the hotel's gardens and the restaurant level of La Frégate, and entered a small sitting room which led to the bar. Being built on a terraced hillside overlooking the town, the restaurant was one floor down from the main entrance. So they climbed the main staircase to the front door and reception. Mike greeted the girl behind the counter,

"Morning . . ."

"Good morning, Sir."

"Phff . . . If you have come up that path every morning. You must be the fittest hotel staff in Europe."

"We come by car" said the girl with a knowing look.

"Could we have some coffee?"

"On the terrace?"

"Please. For three."

"Your room number?"

"Eight."

"Thank you."

Trying to sound as innocent as possible Mike then added, "We come from Brighton. Do you get many people from the South Coast of England?"

"Not really. Most of our customers are businessmen from the big cities." After a pause "Of course, there is Mr Jones from Brighton. He comes at the end of each month to go to the Bank at the bottom of the hill." The girl continued to think aloud, "He is the only one."

"Ralli Brothers?"

"No. The German bank, The Central Park and Commercial."

"Perhaps we'll bump into him one day." Again Mike attempted a nonchalant air.

They walked out to the terrace and inspected an enormous geranium growing out of a sawn-off tree trunk. Mervyn excused himself. He arrived back at exactly the same moment that the girl from reception came from the kitchen carrying a tray of coffee.

When she had gone Mike sighed "Well that doesn't get us very far, does it? *Jones* indeed! He might as well be called *Smith* or *Brown* there is no chance that we will find him in a place like Brighton. And the bank on the corner certainly won't tell us anything, they'll be as discreet as the gnomes of Zurich. If only we knew the name of his company. I daren't ask the girl again or she will suspect something."

"I've got the name of the company" said Mervyn very quietly.

"How did you do that?" said Anna with wide eyes.

"I got it just now while the girl was getting the coffee. I only had a quick glance. The book was at an angle so I couldn't see it clearly, the company was either *Christian Rouffignac* or *Guls and Le Cutte*." This time Mervyn tried his hand at the French pronounciation but with little success.

Over coffee they agreed that the clue which had brought them to Guernsey referred to *La Frégate*, but

93

because they had looked for a boat they had missed the chance to confront the mysterious Mr Jones. The decision to return to Kings Nympton was inevitable; nothing more could be gained by staying. Mervyn's anxiety that he would be stopped and arrested by the police on the way home, was partly relieved by Anna, who persuaded him that he would feel less conspicuous if he bought some new clothes and looked more like a holiday maker. Mike added that the authorities would be looking for him trying to leave the country, and that it would be quite safe to go in the opposite direction.

Mike and Anna's overnight cases were quickly packed and their bills settled before they drove down the hill to the seafront. At the bottom of St Julian's Avenue, Mike stopped the car for a moment to get the exact name of the bank, which the receptionist thought was visited by Mr Jones. Taking a piece of paper from a pocket he carefully wrote, *Zentralspark-asse und Kommerzial Bank of Munich*. Mike then suggested that he and Anna should get a breath of fresh air, while Mervyn packed and bought new clothing. So they dropped him outside the hotel and drove to the far end of Galtegny Esplanade, eventually parking at a spot that looked out over Belle Greve Bay.

It was still a hot cloudless day; the changing tide had brought a refreshing breeze from the sea. They parked in front of a house called *Sea for breakfast*, which made them laugh as they crossed the road to walk along the beach. They reached the edge of the sea, at that moment when it looks as if a huge monster might surface in the waves. But as they broke on the beach the twenty square yards of water erupted into a boiling mass of spume and spray and a large shoal of small fry twisted and turned just below the surface. A dozen gulls seemed prepared for the shoal and noisily gorged themselves while the tiny fish remained in the shallows. When they had gone, the gulls settled back on the water like well fed ducks on an ornamental lake, preening and waiting, expecting to be fed again.

The breeze suddenly dropped, and momentarily all other movement seemed to cease. Very few craft were under sail; most people were lying, on the beach or on the deck of their boats soaking in the midday sun. The sudden stillness hung with menacing heaviness, as if preceding a storm. The crew of a small yacht, about a mile off shore, used the doldrums as an excuse for a pre-lunch swim. They jumped and splashed about, the water amplifying their shrill cries, to create strident waves of sound that disturbed the peace.

"All hands to dance and skylark" said Anna.

"Sorry?"

"Skylark – that is where it comes from – it's an old naval order."

"You will have to explain." Mike looked quite blank.

"It's a naval command. On long voyages, especially if the crew was getting mutinous, the Captain would order. 'All hands to dance and skylark.' That is what they are doing over there from that small boat – skylarking. It was in the book, I was reading, about Victor Hugo."

"Oh." Mike placed a hand on his brow as the omission dawned on him. "We haven't visited his house. I'd quite forgotten I'm afraid."

"It doesn't matter. It is important to get home. If we could only find Mr Jones quickly we might begin to solve the mystery."

"We must get home, but I shouldn't have forgotten about Victor Hugo's house." Mike looked apologetic.

"Will you tell the police what we have discovered?"

"Yes. I am going to ask Mervyn to come back to the cottage and I will phone Sergeant Williams to see if he will meet us there. I'll explain why Mervyn couldn't possibly have done the shooting and then tell him about *La Frégate* and Mr Jones. I think we should be home by mid afternoon and after we've seen the police there should still be time to start looking for the company Mr Jones' works for."

Mike looked at his watch. "We must think about meeting Mervyn. It's almost the time when we said we would pick him up."

As they walked back to the car, the breeze from the sea started to blow again and the possibility of a storm seemed to vanish as quickly as it had come.

The nearer they drove towards the centre of St Peter Port, the more the promenade filled with groups of holiday makers drifting aimlessly; occasionally stopping to look in a window, read a poster or lean on the harbour railings to gaze at someone doing the most ordinary piece of housework on a boat. Trippers queued at the kiosk for tickets to cross to Sark and a newspaper seller joked with the crowd as he sold the lunchtime edition of the island's evening newspaper. A placard by his stand said "Frigate visits town". Mike stopped the car and was about to ask Anna to buy a copy when Mervyn suddenly emerged from the crowd, opened the rear door of the Sierra and jumped in. As he threw a tote bag across to the vacant seat behind Mike he said, "I thought that head-line would catch your eye."

It was immediately obvious why they hadn't noticed Mervyn standing next to the newspaper seller. He had changed his clothes completely. Visiting the local branch of *Next* or *Benneton*, he had purchased a pair of baggy cotton trousers, trainers and a T-shirt with the mysterious announcement "Frogs International".

Mervyn unfolded the newspaper and read aloud "A British Leander Class Frigate arrived in Guernsey this morning on a two-day courtesy visit. The crew expect to play a local team at football."

"I am glad it didn't arrive earlier" said Mike "or we

could have wasted a lot of time looking for you in the wrong place."

"That's what I thought" grunted Mervyn.

Anna turned in her seat to face him "I don't think anyone will spot you dressed like that."

"I hope you're right" Mervyn settled back into his seat, as the car started to climb Le Val des Terres which took them out of St Peter Port and onto the road to the airport. They were in time to catch the midday plane home.

Nobody looked twice at Mervyn as they passed through Immigration at Gatwick. Passengers from the Channel Islands are not required to use passports and normally have unhindered access to the country. But an official seemed to be doing a special check and said to Mike. "Where have you come from today, Sir?"

In a gesture that included them all Mike said "From Guernsey. We were there for a little bit of business and pleasure." They were all waved through the barrier. On the way to the baggage re-claim area, Mike turned to Mervyn and said airily, "Well, welcome home! I am going to phone the police and get Sgt. Williams to meet us at the cottage. We won't let you out of our sight until he is convinced you had nothing to do with the shooting."

Mervyn looked anxious "It has got to be done, so we might as well get it over with as quickly as possible."

"I am also going to give the police the other information we have discovered about La Frégate and Mr Jones." Mike paused "And you will have to tell him where you got the clue about La Frégate and we'll need to explain how we all misread it as '*a frigate*'."

"Mmm" muttered Mervyn who was lost in thought. Coming back to the present situation he said, "And then what will we do?"

"Find Mr Jones" said Anna. "He's the key to every-thing."

"Here's a phone." Mike had stopped by a British Telecom box. He turned and looked up at a bank of T.V. monitors. "There is our flight – GE403 – the baggage is on carousel four. I will meet you up there in a moment."

Mervyn and Anna took the escalator while Mike phoned Brighton police station. Sgt. Williams said he would leave straightaway and meet them at Kings Nympton.

Once upstairs in the baggage re-claim area, Mike found Mervyn and Anna who had already put their bags on a trolley. They passed swiftly through the arrivals hall to the car park, found their car and headed up the motorway towards home.

When the South Downs loomed ahead, Mike left the A27, turning west just past Albourne. After the landscape of Guernsey which resembled a vast kitchen garden, it was good to see the lush, rambling excellence of Sussex. Oak and chestnut gave substance to the scene; while blue bell, campion, speedwell and buttercup added colour. What remained of an avenue of hornbean acted as the reminder that man had tried to subdue this land for centuries. The short flight from the Channel Islands to the South Coast had transported them from one world to another.

Mike braked at the sight of a home-made notice reading "Danger! Fox cubs at play."

They passed a sloping green bank grazed by a nanny goat; the radius of her freedom measured about twelve feet and was secured by a heavy metal stake. The perfect circle of grass that had been eaten would have delighted Euclides. The goat had been moved regularly and the circles of already consumed grass, marked the hillside with a motif reminiscent of the Olympic Games.

Suddenly, just past New Timber, Kings Nympton lay peacefully below them in the afternoon sunlight.

The Dragon's Back

Slowly circling high above the village, like a sinister gathering of vultures, were half a dozen hangliders riding the thermals that rose on the northerly edge of the Downs. Their presence seemed to be a portent. Was the mystery about to be solved or was another crime about to be committed?

Chapter 9

The car turned from Kissing Tree Lane into the road that ran along the edge of the Green. Once around the corner they could see Sgt. Williams waiting outside the cottage. As Mike stopped the car, Mervyn quickly opened his door, stepped out and marched across to him. "I think you are looking for me."

After a quick bold glance at the policeman, all Mervyn could do was to look down at his feet. He felt guilty and had the same sinking feeling that he used to have at school, when called into the headmaster's study.

"Yes. I would like a word, Sir. About the death of Mr Thraxter."

Mike joined them. "Why don't we go inside? It will be much more comfortable and certainly more private." One or two people on the other side of the Green peered through the windows of their cottages. Several recognised Sgt. Williams as the policeman who had visited the village after the shooting and wondered if he had come to make an arrest.

Mike led the way into his cottage, seated them and then telephoned through to *The Old Nail Shot* for coffee to be brought across. Anna was the first to speak. "Sergeant. The evidence shows that Mervyn couldn't have done the shooting."

"I see."

Anna continued "We were with Malcolm when he died. It was about 2.30 and in Brighton there is a man called Orage who will confirm that Mervyn was with him at the time."

"I think I ought to hear what Mr Lyle has to say, thank you, Madam." The Sergeant paused and opened a notebook. "Now Sir. How would you describe your movements on the day of Malcolm Thraxter's death?"

"I went to Brighton, then to Gatwick."

"How did you get into Brighton, Sir?"

"Malcolm drove me in the car."

"What time was your flight?"

"5 o'clock."

"Then why didn't Mr Thraxter wait and take you to Gatwick?"

"I wanted him to come back here to finish a table that was due to be collected at 6 o'clock. I knew I could easily get to Gatwick by train."

"Wouldn't it be nearer the truth to say that you decided to go to Gatwick after the shooting, as a way of getting out of the country quickly?"

"*No.* It had nothing to do with Malcolm's death. I had planned to go to Gatwick. That is why I went to Brighton; to borrow money for an air ticket."

"And where were you going?"

"Guernsey."

"For any particular reason?"

"Yes. I was trying to find the man who sold cocaine to my sister. Malcolm discovered he would be in St Peter Port."

"I see. And where did Mr Thraxter get this information?"

"I don't know."

"Not very helpful Sir. And how did *you* get it?"

"A note – Malcolm gave it to me."

"It said?"

"Well I thought it said . . ."

"Sergeant," Mike interrupted, "Apparently the note said 'La Frégate St Peter Port'. At first we all thought it meant 'a frigate in St Peter Port' so we were all looking in the wrong place."

The Sergeant turned back to Mervyn. "Is that right – can you confirm that?"

"I can do better," said Mervyn. "I've got the note." He took his wallet from a hip pocket, found a piece of paper and unfolded it before putting it on the coffee table in front of them. It appeared to be a page torn from a "telephone message" pad. Printed at the top was the company's name with a slogan at the bottom. In a fairly legible hand someone had scribbled *"La Frégate St. Peter Port."*

"Did you find the man you were looking for?" the Sergeant continued.

"No."

"But he is called *Jones* and he stayed at La Frégate" said Anna.

"Oh come now Miss. Surely it was 'Mr & Mrs Jones'? Isn't that the name they always use in a hotel?"

It all sounded too futile: how were they to look for the elusive "Mr Jones". It was so obviously a made-up name.

"Mmm", the Sergeant grunted; shook his head once or twice and put his notebook away before turning to Mervyn. "I want you to come back to Brighton and make a statement. The airline ought to be able to confirm that you were on their passenger list and someone should be able to testify that you were in Guernsey. Your car was found abandoned in Bournemouth, so I think for the moment, that eliminates you from our enquiries."

"You mean that I will be free after I have made the statement?" The relief on Mervyn's face was obvious.

"Yes."

"Boy. I thought I was going to be on a murder charge. All the papers said I was at Gatwick straight after the shooting and I knew I couldn't prove that I didn't get there until 4 o'clock."

"I shouldn't always believe what you read in the newspapers, Sir." The Sergeant smiled for the first time.

The four of them stood, moved towards the door and had just concluded their "goodbyes" when the coffee arrived. It was declined by the Sergeant who said he ought to get back to Brighton and he left with Mervyn.

Once the room was quiet again Mike poured Anna a cup of coffee and handing it to her said, "If only we had realised earlier that it was *La Frégate* and hadn't wasted all that time looking for a boat."

"I would hate to have missed Le Nautique and our breakfast at La Frégate."

"True," said Mike already lost in thought.

"What next?"

"The only chance we have of finding Mr Jones is to try and trace the company he works for. Mike crossed to his desk in the far side of the room, and took a telephone directory from a drawer. After a few moments he said "Well . . . There isn't a 'Christian Rouffignac' or 'Guls and Le Cutte' listed. I think we will have to go into Brighton and check at the Library. If these companies exist, they will be in Kelly's, or the Chamber of Commerce Directory."

He gathered up the used coffee cups and as he put them back on the tray, he saw the note Mervyn had taken from his wallet.

"Mervyn's forgotten this." He waved it in Anna's direction. The name at the top was in large Chinese characters. The bottom line was in English and in much smaller type, it said "Soho's main supplier for Chinese cuisine." Without looking at it properly Mike put it in his pocket.

Crossing the Downs, Mike and Anna followed Dyke Road Avenue towards the centre of Brighton. The wide avenue soon gave way to the more suburban end of Dyke Road which eventually became the shops and department stores of North Street.

They circled part of the Steine with George IV's Royal Pavilion on their left. The name, which suggests some sort of summer residence, hardly does the building justice. History can have seen few *love-nests* more sumptuous than the Pavilion with its bizarre chinoisie interiors and facades of onion domes and minarets. It is easy to agree with Sidney Smith who said "It looked as though the dome of St Paul's had come down to Brighton and pupped." Mike and Anna managed to park nearby and walking through the gardens past the Dome they entered the town's library.

The doorway led into a lobby tiled with dark green *art nouveau* tiles, and hanging above the staircase was Benjamin Wilson's portrait of Richard Russell.

Mike pointed it out, "That's the doctor who wrote about the benefits of drinking and swimming in sea water."

The picture revealed a colourless old man in a dark coat and a grey wig, with shrunken cheeks and shrewd eyes.

"He doesn't look a very good advertisement to me."

Mike laughed "Well the fashionable hyperchondriacs in London were soon buying bottles of 'Brighthelmstone water' as pancea for all their ills."

There were three girls at the information point in the Library. Mike spoke to the first, an almost albino blonde, dressed in punk style clothing with jewellery to match.

"I need to check on one or two local businesses. Is it er . . . mm Kelly's Business Directory that I need?"

"Yes. It's over there." The blonde pointed.

"And the Chamber of Commerce Directory?" said Anna.

"No. Kompass Company Information is what you want. They're both just there." The blonde continued to point in a vague way, while looking at lines of green type that had suddenly started to appear on a VDU screen.

They found the books and carried them to an empty table. Mike opened a large volume and started to study it, occasionally grunting to himself and sometimes quickly turning over the pages to look at a different section. He tried the other books and finally said "Nothing here I'm afraid, nothing remotely like the names that Mervyn saw at La Frégate."

Anna sighed "Which means we still don't really have anything to go on."

"Not a thing." Mike paused "Except I still have the note that Malcolm gave to Mervyn." He found it in his pocket, unfolded it, and put it on the table.

"Whatever it says we can't read it. The most important bit's in Chinese – so it doesn't help." As if searching for inspiration he read aloud the line printed at the bottom "Soho's main supplier for Chinese Cuisine."

"But we know who can read it." Anna was wide-eyed with the realisation.

"Who?"

"Your vicar. He obviously has an interest in China and said he studied Chinese."

"Right."

"Let's give him a try."

The books were returned to their shelves and they drove back to Kings Nympton.

Within half an hour they were being shown into the vicar's study.

"My dear," Mrs Hoskins addressed her husband, "Mr Main and Miss Richardson would like a word." Having opened the front door of the vicarage a few moments earlier, she now ushered them into her husband's study which appeared to be even untidier than before. There were more bulging cardboard boxes, which served as a precarious prop for a black plastic sack sealed with sellotape and labelled "Knitted blankets for refugees". And there was just room for a pile of bright scarlet books entitled *"Redemption Hymnal"* which were the gift of Hallelujah Harry. He had found them in a second hand book shop in Brighton and thought that they would put a bit of life into the parish eucharist.

The vicar was at his desk reading and researching for his Sunday sermon and making notes on a large pad balanced on his knees. The reference books were perched on a desk already overflowing with papers.

"Oh do come in. How n . . . nice to see you." The vicar turned and smiled, but as usual looked over the top of his glasses at the ceiling.

"We hate to disturb you," said Anna.

"Any excuse to leave my s . . . s . . . sermuncle is always most welcome." He used the anglicised Latin word as if it were still in common use.

"I thought vicars enjoyed making sermons," said Anna slightly shocked by the revelation.

"Alas, not me. I don't mind s . . . saying a prayer, but the endless need to s . . . say something relevant and interesting – terrifies me."

Mike advanced with Malcolm's note. "You were so very helpful about the K'ang Hsi vases – we wondered if you could translate this?"

The vicar took the piece of paper "What do you want to know?"

"The Chinese writing at the top . . . we presumed it is a name?"

"That's correct."

"What does it say?"

"Taiping."

"That's what Malcolm said before he died."

"Taiping Supermarket."

"Did you say *typing* Supermarket." Mike looked as though he doubted the vicar.

"No. Not what you do with a typewriter. It is T-A-I-P-I-N-G." The vicar spelt it out. "Taiping means 'great peace', as typhoon means 'great wind'. Actually the Chinese words are *tai fung*. In English we have changed it to typhoon."

"So it's the *Great Peace* Supermarket." Mike finally unravelled what the vicar was saying.

"Exactly."

"No wonder we couldn't find it in Brighton."

"Indeed as you can see from the bottom of the page it's in Soho." The piece of paper was handed back to Mike.

"That's marvellous," said Anna, "Once again you have been a great help."

"How is the search going for the young man's killer?" The vicar changed the subject.

"Not well I'm afraid." Mike shrugged.

"Every clue, eventually seems to peter out and leads us nowhere" added Anna.

"And the dwarfs . . . have you been able to link them with the murder?" As on other occasions the vicar's stutter vanished once he became absorbed in the conversation.

"Not really." Mike paused as if in thought "Although I think I saw one the other night."

"Mmm . . . I still feel they are a separate issue." The vicar steepled his hands as if in prayer and glanced down at the notes he had been making.

"We ought to leave you," said Mike, "We will try Soho and see if the *Great Peace Supermarket* reveals anything about the mysterious Mr Jones."

The vicar had started writing again, but looked up to say "the Chinese bit of Soho is just north of Leicester

Square – that's where I go to get my Wunton skins and Five Spices powder."

As they stepped out of his study, Mrs Hoskins reappeared and showed them out. They asked her to thank the vicar for sparing the time to see them.

Back in the study the Reverend Mr Hoskins was once more immersed in the Greek of the New Testament. He smiled to himself as he wrote "seeing they were *agramatoi kai idiotai* – uneducated common men."

Mike and Anna drove to Gatwick to catch the *Express* to Victoria. The frequent non-stop service made it a popular way for the villagers of Kings Nymptom to get into London avoiding the traffic jams of the early evening. Not only did they have the comfort of modern rolling stock, they also had other luxuries not found on the commuter trains, such as telephones and a bar-trolley. British Rail's aim was to woo the international traveller on his arrival in England, but the inhabitants of Sussex weren't slow to use the amenities for themselves.

As Mike and Anna settled into opposite seats, their eyes met, smiling and holding a reassurance of tenderness. Mike moved across to sit next to Anna. Since breakfast, he had wanted to say something and that briefly held look, gave him the freedom to speak.

Suddenly they both started to talk at once.

"I have a . . ."

"Do tell me . . ."

"Sorry."

"Sorry."

"Please go on" Mike made the gentlemanly gesture.

"I was going to ask about your wife."

"Claire?"

"Yes."

"What can I say?"

"What sort of person was she?"

"Tall ... dark ... gifted ... gentle ... I miss her."

"Gifted?"

"A pianist. She played in the local Chamber Orchestra until her final operation. I sometimes feel guilty that I miss her music as much as I miss her."

"Isn't that the same thing?"

"I suppose it is. I find it difficult to know how people can live without music."

"I feel the same about art. I find houses without pictures are soul-less."

"That is a good description. They are important to me too." Mike took Anna's hand.

"What sort of music do you enjoy?" she asked.

"That's difficult. Almost anything."

"Opera? Jazz?"

"I have only just started listening to opera. I am not up to the really heavy stuff like Wagner, but I like almost anything especially Mozart. I like jazz too, but at heart I suppose I am a Brahms and Mahler fan – does that mean anything?"

"It means you're a romantic."

"I suppose it does."

"And you're not religious – I find that interesting."

"Are the two things connected?"

"Often."

"I go to church occasionally. Most people in the village do. Since Claire's death I've wanted to add religion to art and music, because, as you have just said there seems to be a connection. But ..." Mike hesitated.

"Yes?"

"Church has always been a problem." Mike paused. "Although Claire seemed to find something before she died, in the last few weeks she completely changed. She was at peace with everybody – with me, the doctor and nurses, even her illness. In her last hours, instead of declining, she became radiant. That's the only way I can put it."

"She got help, but not from the church? Is that what you are saying?"

"N ... No ..." Mike wasn't quite sure what he wanted to say. Anna waited for him to continue. He drew a deep breath and expelled it loudly. "I suppose in the past church has always appeared to me, to be a bit of a charade. But there are a few people in the village who aren't playing at all. For them, it seems to be genuine."

"They're not churchgoers?"

"Yes, they are – but somehow they're different. There are two women who helped Claire after her last operation. They – well studied with her I suppose. That's what helped her."

"It worked for them because they are women, but it can't work for you because your a man?"

"No that's not what I mean. I'm not managing to express it very well. There are two families really. The husbands work in the City at Lloyd's and go to church near there on a Tuesday. It seems to have made things real for them and now their wives are involved too. The husbands have asked me to meet them once a week for a bible study, before they go off to the City. I'm thinking about it. I'm not sure I can get up that early."

Anna changed the subject "An interesting trilogy – art, music and religion – and no food. Isn't that surprising?"

"Food is important. What Samuel Johnson said about London is true of food. 'Anyone bored with food is bored with life.' That's what food is about – life; it feeds the body. Whereas art and music are *soul* food and feed the spirit. I haven't thought about it before, but that's what religion is meant to do, and presumably does, when its real."

"Is that what you were going to say just now?" Anna looked at him.

"No. I was going to say that I have a problem."

"What's that?"

"I think I'm becoming more than a little fond of you."

"I think I have the same problem."

They were brought suddenly and sharply back to earth by the Guard's announcement that they were arriving at Victoria. But the previous moments admission meant that no intrusion, however prosaic, could snatch away the growing confidence that Mike and Anna were finding in one another.

They took the Victoria line tube to Green Park and changed for Leicester Square where they were thrust out into a busy Charing Cross Road. On reaching ground level, Anna had caught sight of the street sign and the phrase "84 Charing Cross Road" had come into her mind. After only a few paces they turned sharply into *Newport Court* and all thoughts of Helen Hanff and present day London immediately vanished. They entered a lane that could have been almost anywhere in the Far East.

Now, even the familiar London street signs were printed in Chinese and the tables of Wing Wah's coffee shop spilled out onto the pavement where you could enjoy "Red bean sweet with ice" or "Iced Kaching" to your heart's content. Enormous durians were piled high outside Ping Wu's greengrocery, looking like cannon ball-sized sweet chestnuts. By the time they reached Gerrard Street they felt as if they had entered a Chinese City; the fish stall displayed *Venus Clams* and *Thunder Bream* while the restaurant windows were full of *Peking Duck*. The only clue that they were still in England, were the heavily disguised British Telecom boxes. Hiding beneath bright red pagoda roofs, the word "Telephone" printed in mock Chinese characters, finally gave them away.

Gerrard Street had been turned into a pedestrian precinct, traffic being barred at each end by a carved wooden arch rather like an enormous oriental "Pi" sign. The upright supports and overlapping cross-bar were heavily decorated with Chinese characters and heraldic devices.

They passed under the arch at the Cambridge Circus end of Gerrard Street and found the *TAIPING SUPERMARKET*, about halfway along on the left hand side. The shop had a central doorway with display windows on either side. One window was full of food imported from Hong Kong and the other displayed Chinese Cooking implements. Everything was there, from the ubiquitous wok to the utilitarian cleaver, and even decorations that would give the authentic touch of the East to restaurants as far apart as Bristol and Barnsley. At the centre of this window was an exhibition of K'ang Hsi vases and behind them an enlarged reproduction of an early Chinese print, showing artists and designers producing various items in porcelain. These vases were "Authentic copies of a famous 17th Century vase", at least, so the print firmly announced.

As they entered they couldn't help noticing a pungent oriental smell, a Chinese young man approached them "Can I help you?" At first they were surprised by his strong East London accent and the absence of the breathless lisp associated with the Hollywood stereotype.

"We are interested in the K'ang Hsi vases in the window. Would it be possible to tell us where they come from?" Mike was aware that it would be difficult to get out of the shop quickly if they had to.

"From China. We buy them from a supplier in Hong Kong. Why do you ask?"

"It sounds rather melodramatic but we are looking

for someone who killed a friend. It was in Brighton and K'ang Hsi vases were involved."

"You should go to the police."

"We have, but they don't seem to be making much progress." Mike took Malcolm's note from his pocket. "Does this mean anything?"

"We give them to our customers."

"The pads?"

"Yes."

"Do you have any customers in Brighton or Hove?"

"No. We mainly supply the London area and the Midlands."

"Are you sure?"

"Absolutely."

A phone had started to ring behind the counter. The young man offered the note back to Mike "I've got to go; we're short-staffed today." Mike was determined to ask one more question, so he hesitated slightly before taking the note. "What about customers in Guernsey?"

"You've got to be joking," said the young man as he picked up the phone. He held a hand over the mouth piece. "What, a place like that?"

"Like what?"

"La Frégate." In spite of the accent, which was straight out of the Whitechapel Road, he managed to pronounce the name of the hotel without any difficulty. But he brought the conversation to an end by speaking into the telephone. "Taiping. Yes ... two dozen bottles ... OK ... tomorrow ... one gross? ... yes ... fifty ... OK ... OK."

Mike and Anna left the shop. Once outside they turned right and took a few paces until they were out of the young man's view.

"That was *very* interesting," said Mike.

"Very."

"There is certainly some connection with La Frégate."

"Yes." Anna had her back to the road. "Don't turn around now" she said "But the young man is taking the K'ang Hsi vases out of the window."

"And don't you turn around either," said Mike, "The taxi that has just gone past had Mr and Mrs Wayne Lane as passengers and it's stopping. Let's get away from here quickly." Mike and Anna hurried back toward Leicester Square Tube Station.

If they had stayed, they would have seen that the taxi didn't stop outside the *TAIPING SUPERMARKET*, but next door, which was a small lock-up shop declaring itself to be *RINGMASTER ACTS – Agents for the smallest and best circus entertainers in the world.* A metal security grill was pulled down inside the window and wedged in front of it, a notice that read *"PROPERTY FOR SALE – Immediate vacant possession."*

Wayne Lane stepped close to the window, and using a hand to stop the reflection, peered inside. He could see through the largest diamond-shaped links of the security curtain and saw that the window was filled with a large *papier mâché* model of Niagara Falls. A tightrope was suspended above the famous 150 foot high cascades. On it a highwire walker was making his way across, pushing a man in a wheelbarrow. Below, on both the American and Canadian sides of the river, above the falls, a large crowd watched with bated breath. In the foreground a card said *"Jean Francois Gravelet, who worked under the name of BLONDIN making his way across the river Niagara in 1858."*

Wayne Lane moved to the door. This time, the security grill was outside and was firmly padlocked at ground level. He looked at Chelsea-Ann, turned up the collar of his raincoat and shrugged. They both

hurried away in the direction of Piccadilly Circus Tube
station.

Chapter 10

Anna arrived at Mike's cottage the following morning. As she stepped from her car, closing the door with a bang, a clamour of rooks rose noisily from the trees in the vicarage garden. They smudged the morning sky like a swirl of tealeaves at the bottom of a cup. Anna knocked at the front door of the cottage, but there was no answer, so she returned to her car to wait.

She had picked up her newspaper as she left Roedean, and now retrieved it from the passenger seat glancing at the headline "Chancellor's Cautious Optimism". The main front page article was full of city jargon about the Government's monetary policy and their fiscal-fencing. It held no interest for Anna, so she turned to the back page and tackled the cross-word, filling in the blank squares with practised ease. "A Royal Marine orchestra as may be seen on the sleeve" quickly became "ARMBAND"; and a "Musicians go slow movement" exactly filled five squares as "LARGO". At this point Mike and Mervyn emerged from *The Den of Antiquity*, and seeing Anna, hurried across the Green towards her.

"Sorry I wasn't here when you arrived" Mike apologised. "Mervyn has found another note from Malcolm so I went to see what it said."

Mervyn beamed, held it up, shrugged his shoulders

and then raised his hands in despair. "Again we don't know what it means, but it must mean something because Malcolm put it under my blotter and he knew that was where I put important reminders." He shrugged again, "Anyway I'm off to see Harry to try and find out where he got the vase from." Waving goodbye, he set off towards the vicarage next door which was sandwiched between Mike's cottage and the parish church of St Rumon.

Mike opened the door of Anna's car to help her out. She hesitated, still working at the crossword. "I need *six down*: 'Checks and polishes repeatedly.' Seven letters?"

"Please don't ask me. I don't have the tortuous mind necessary for word games. Come and have a cup of coffee while we make some plans?"

Anna was still muttering to herself, "checks and polishes repeatedly" as they sat down in the sitting room of the cottage. Mike phoned for coffee.

Two very friendly Siamese cats bounded in from the cottage kitchen. "May I introduce?" said Mike with a grand gesture "Badinage and Persiflage, my two companions – you may call them 'Bad' and 'Percy' – everybody does." They were already making friends with Anna, as with arched backs and rigid tails they vied noisily for her attention.

"They're just back from the cattery" explained Mike. "I put them there while I was away. I'm in their bad books because I didn't stay to look after them. Claire had a passion for Siamese, so they've always been part of the family."

"They're marvellous, but what a strange noise? They don't sound like other cats?"

"Some people argue that they aren't, but a species of exceptionally intelligent beings from another planet. That's how Claire thought of them."

The coffee arrived from the kitchen.

Mervyn found Hallelujah Harry near the outbuildings at the back of the vicarage. He was tinkering with the vicar's lawn mower. He had adjusted the blades of the grass cutter, having sharpened them in preparation for another day's work on the seemingly endless expanse of vicarage grass. Because Harry was such a familiar sight in the village it didn't occur to Mervyn to think about the incongruity of the scene. Yet it presented an almost irreconcilable picture. Harry in flower-power-come-western dress, complete with John Lennon hairstyle and spectacles to match, set against a quintessentially English backdrop of a vicarage garden amidst the rolling Downs of Sussex.

"Morning Harry."

" 'Ello Mr Lyle. I thought the police had got you."

"They let me go."

"More furniture to be moved?"

"No. It's the Chinese vase."

"You want one?"

"No. I want to know where you got it."

"Oh I can't tell you that Mr Lyle."

"Why?"

"It's private."

"You mean you pinched it?"

"No. Nobody owned it: it was just lying around."

"You *nicked* it. That's what I said."

"Well if you put it like that I suppose I did. But nobody seemed to want it."

"Where did you get it?"

"I can't say Mr Lyle, 'onest I can't."

"Why?"

"Well, as I said, it's private."

"Harry there's been a murder."

"I know."

"You know the trouble you had with the police in America?"

"What's that got to do with it?"

118

"There's a connection Harry, between the vase and
the murder."

"What?"

"Well I don't know. I wouldn't be asking your 'elp if
I knew. You told the vicar I gave you the vase."

"No I didn't Mr Lyle."

"Well 'e says you did."

"He asked me if you gave it to me. I didn't actually
say 'yes' – I sort of agreed."

"That means we're both implicated."

"I suppose it does."

" 'Course it does."

"So Harry *where* did you get it from?"

"A shed Mr Lyle."

"Harreee! *which* shed?"

"The one at the bottom of Mr Keating's garden."

"Max Keating?"

"Yer."

"You found the vase there?"

"That's where I found the *vases* Mr Lyle."

"Thank you Harry. At last I think this is the information we've been looking for."

"You won't tell 'im."

"No I won't tell him. Thanks."

As Mervyn moved away, Harry added to the incongruity of the scene by saying "Have a nice day!"

"You bet 'arry. You bet." But Mervyn wasn't really
thinking about what he was saying, his mind was on
other things.

Anna stood and gathered up her things ready to leave.
"I passed a new restaurant in Kemp Town last night.
A vegetarian one called – 'Oat Cuisine'."

"I like it. They deserve to succeed with a name like
that."

"Do you think they won't?"

"They wouldn't have done a few years ago. It's too much like pushing your prejudices on other people."

"We all have prejudices about food?"

"Yes. But in this business you can't afford to let them show. I just serve people what they want; I'm not responsible for their taste. If I only served the dishes I liked, I would soon go out of business. Would you like to try Kemp Town for lunch?"

"No thanks. It was only the name that took my fancy." Anna bent down to pick up her newspaper which had fallen underneath her chair. Somewhere in her subconscious she was again struggling with the clue "Checks and polishes repeatedly". On a conscious level she looked at Mike and continued "My meeting should be finished by 12.30. I think it's only a matter of sorting out the exam timetable. Shall we meet outside the Library at Roedean at a quarter to one?"

"Fine." Mike saw Anna to her car, opened the door and let her in. " 'Till lunchtime."

"Bye."

"The car sped away and stopped almost immediately. Anna reversed and wound down her window. "I've just realised 'Checks and polishes repeatedly' is 'REBUFFS'."

"Did you stop just to say that?"

"No. I've also realised that *Guls and Le Cutte* is an anagram of *The Slug and Lettuce.*"

Somewhere in the undergrowth behind the vicarage a pheasant coughed with hollow laughter as it hurried away, both Mike and Anna felt a sense of mockery in the bird's scornful cry.

Chapter 11

Mike had watched Anna circle the Green and head up Kissing Tree Lane to Brighton before he turned back towards the cottage. He had intended going inside to deal with the mail and look at the draft menus for the next few days, before setting out to Kemp Town to collect her for lunch. Now he hesitated. He thought of the implausibility of Max Keating being involved in Malcolm's death.

It then occurred to him, that there was no better time than the present to catch Max for a brief moment, before *The Slug and Lettuce* opened its doors for the onslaught of the lunchtime trade. So, without going back inside, he crossed the Green to the village pub.

The door was already ajar when he arrived and his knocking caused it to swing open wider still. As there was no response, he stepped inside.

"Max are you there?"

There was a heady mixture of both stale and fresh beer smells in the bar. Someone had recently connected a new barrel in the cellar and drawn the beer up to the bar to test its clarity thus making sure it was unsullied enough for the meticulous standards of the lunchtime crowd. The only movement to catch his eye was a curl of smoke from a newly lighted cigarette resting on an ashtray next to a half empty tankard of

121

ale. Whoever was setting up the bar, couldn't be far away.

"Max? Have you got a moment?"

The door to the cellar was open and a light glowed from below. Mike presumed that whoever was down there, couldn't hear him calling up in the bar, so he climbed down the wide-stepped staircase that traversed the west wall of the cellar. Descending the steps he thought how curious it was that a building not originally designed as a public house should have such a spacious cellar. It wouldn't have been out of place, in one of the great houses of Sussex.

Reaching the uneven stone-flagged floor, he called out, "Max?"

The light was dim and his eyes had to adjust to the darkness. His heart missed a beat when he realised that a dwarf was standing about ten feet away in the shadows of one of the recesses in the cellar. He was dressed in jeans and a sweater and standing with his feet firmly apart, he held a pick-axe handle in a raised hand, ready to strike. His complexion was sallow and his dark hair combed forward. A beard grew from below his chin, but the rest of his face was clean shaven. His eyebrows fluttered like two large moths. In spite of his lack of stature he dredged up a deep basso profundo voice "Come and get me Mr Main."

"So you know who I am?"

"Of course."

At that moment, Mike was aware of a movement just behind him. His reflexes made him duck as he turned away. A dwarf who had been somewhere in the darkest recesses of the cellar, pistol-whipped him with the stock of a sawn-off shot gun. Mike realised that there must be more than one tiny assailant behind him, because as one pair of hands grabbed his arms and pushed them up his back, another clapped a folded handkerchief over his nose and mouth. His final memory as he drifted from consciousness, was the sweet sickly smell of ether.

When he came to, he found that his hands had been firmly tied behind his back and his ankles lashed together with a stout piece of rope. The dwarf, with the pick-axe handle, was sitting on a case of wine keeping guard. On seeing that his eyes were open the others hauled him upright, with as much care as they might show a sack of potatoes. Then dragged him across the floor so that his back was against a wall to keep him erect.

There was a sound of a door slamming overhead. Whoever it was clattered down the cellar stairs. "Blast! Damn you Main! One more day and we would've been away."

"Max? I don't believe it?"

"Well now you know."

"Why?"

"Why does anyone do anything?"

"Yes, but Max . . . Why you?"

"It's a way of earning a crust."

"Whatever you've got stashed away you won't be able to keep. And Malcolm's death means they'll lock you away for years."

"If they catch us."

"They will."

"We've got a place in the sun. New identities. New passports. A secret bank account. Another few hours and we would've been away where nobody could find us." He snarled, his expression grim in the light of a naked bulb hanging a few feet from his head.

"The bank is not a secret. It's in Guernsey – we know that."

"I heard you'd been snooping around. Well it's all been moved to Switzerland. You'll never trace it there."

"Max you're mad. This is England you know – not Panama or Colombia. You'll never get away with it."

"I think we will."

"How does an English publican get mixed up in something like this?"

"When they sent me down from university I discovered that the first principle of business is that you can make an awful lot of money selling people what they want."

"They're drugs Max. They kill people."

Max's fury and frustration seemed to dissolve momentarily as he adopted the pathos of a child caught in some act of innocent truancy. Playing the part, he whined, "Actually it's my family business. I'm only doing what my forebears did, right here, in this village," and adding wistfully, "In this *very* house."

"What do you mean?"

"Many years ago there was a woman in my family called Esme, she married a man called Felix Platter. He made drugs from garden flowers that could stunt human growth. He made a fortune. Together they imported opium for the aristocracy. That's what this cellar was for. It all happened here hundreds of years ago."

"And the dwarfs?"

"Well they're a family trade-mark. As Old Felix Platter made his fortune from them, I thought I'd have a little band as my couriers. They appeal to my gothic sense of horror. The Platters were famous for drugs and contraband – and they will be again."

"Wouldn't *infamous* be a better word. And now you've got to get rid of me."

"We nearly had to do that in Guernsey. I foolishly used Ma's maiden name at La Frégate. I signed the book, 'M A Jones' – would you believe . . . '*Ma* Jones'. I'll never do that again. Our account in Switzerland doesn't have a name, just a number and all the number crunchers in the world won't be able to work out the combination. One more delivery tonight, then I'm away and nobody here will ever see me again. My bosses know that." Any hint of pathos was now abandoned, as the ruthless determination of a criminal mind took charge.

"Your bosses?"

"You don't think that it's just me and 'Ma' do you?"

"I suppose not."

"It's a big consortium. I look after the English end and make sure that the money is nicely laundered in Guernsey." There was a pause as Max returned to the grip of his original fury and spat words at Mike, "You do realise, don't you, that you know far too much. When the helicopter makes the delivery tonight, it'll take you away and deposit you somewhere – out in the Channel. And that will be the end of Mr Michael Main." He turned to the dwarf sitting on the case of wine. "Gag him Bildad and make sure he is secure. We don't want anything to frighten our lunchtime customers do we?"

"Right you are Mr Keating", growled the deep bass voice.

Anna was waiting in her room above the Reference Library at Roedean. She made one or two desultory adjustments to her examination timetable to pass the time, and despite her lack of wholehearted concentration, managed to sort out the notes she needed on Giotto and Masaccio for a series of lessons she was preparing on the development of art in Florence. Her mind was not on what she was doing as she was expecting that at any moment, Mike's car would sweep around Number Four House from the terrace. It never came.

Somewhere around 2 o'clock she phoned the cottage. There was no reply. As the first hint of anxiety began to grow in Anna's mind, she decided to drive to Kings Nympton, and arrived a little after 2.30. Parking outside the cottage she knocked at the front door. The building was deserted again but unlike earlier in the day the emptiness seemed final – as if Mike would never return. There was just a chance that Mervyn might be in, so she crossed the Green towards *The Den of Antiquity*. She did this with a sense of foreboding; the last time she had crossed the Green in that direction, she had been with Mike and they had discovered Malcolm just before he died. As she neared *The Den of Antiquity* she could see Mervyn pottering around in the side window, filling it with Victorian desk sets and paraffin lamps. He turned as she opened the door.

"'ello, Miss Richardson. Mr Main not with you?"

"He seems to have disappeared."

"What?"

"Mike was going to meet me at 12.45 at Roedean but he didn't turn up. Have you seen him?"

"No. The last time I saw him was this morning when I set off to see Harry. Before we saw you we said we might go to see the vicar this afternoon, to sort out the note that Malcolm put under my blotter."

"Could we go and see if he is there?"

"Yer I'll be right with you."

Mervyn locked up and together they recrossed the Green, this time heading for St Rumon's vicarage where they were quickly shown into the vicar's untidy study.

"Ah Miss Richardson and er . . . er Mr Lyle? No Mr Main?"

"We can't find him."

"Has he been here?"

"Were you expecting him *here*?"

"Yes. We found another note from Malcolm this morning. At least this one was in English, but we still can't understand it. It's on the same Chinese paper.

We thought it might have some 'Chinese' meaning you could help us with."

"I see," said the vicar in a way that was obvious that he didn't.

Mervyn took the piece of paper from his pocket. *THE GREAT PEACE SUPERMARKET* was printed at the top in Chinese characters and someone had hurriedly written in capitals, *NEXT DELIVERY – FRIDAY NIGHT – 11 P.M. THE DRAGON'S BACK*. Mervyn passed it to the vicar "Does it mean anything?"

"It is er . . . a Chinese way of describing a specific geographic feature of the countryside. It says that the next delivery is going to be tonight at 11 p.m. on the Dragon's Back."

"I can read that! But what *specific feature* of the countryside?"

"It can be anywhere."

"*What* can be anywhere?"

"Well its er . . . a hill. Yes er . . . a hill . . . the spine of a hill. Any hill . . . anywhere." The vicar paused. "If it was in Kings Nympton it would be . . ." He was momentarily lost in thought as he gazed out of the window towards the Downs.

"Yes?"

"If it was Kings Nympton . . ." The vicar continued to stare out of the window, as if searching for the answer.

"Yes?" Both Anna and Mervyn were glued to the spot waiting for him to speak.

"If it was Kings Nympton . . . it would refer to May Hill. Yes that's what it is . . . an obvious hill with a spine. The Chinese often plant a row of trees along it. It's May Hill . . . 11 o'clock tonight."

Mervyn clenched his teeth and expelling air with great force turned to Anna. "I think we are getting to the heart of the matter. I wonder if Mr Main is one step ahead of us, and that's the trouble?"

"I haven't seen Mr Main today." said the vicar.

As they stepped through the vicarage gate, a car drew up outside Mike Main's cottage; it was the two Americans. Wayne Lane recognised Anna and came towards them. "Hi there. We're looking for Mike. Is he at home today?"

"I am afraid not." Anna answered firmly, "We can't find him anywhere."

"Really?"

"Did you want him for something that is important?"

"Yes I think it is." The American seemed reticent to continue and then changed his mind. "We have been deceiving you, I'm afraid, we are police officers."

"I told you so." Mervyn smiled with obvious delight that he had been right.

"We are N.Y.P.D. Narcotics Bureau." Wayne Lane showed his *New York Police Department* shield instead of a warrant card. "Chelsea-Ann isn't my wife; she's police officer Chelsea-Ann Ferrari. At a conference this noon, we decided that you're all in great danger if you keep poking at this particular can of worms. So we came to warn you, unofficially, to steer clear for a few days. The news on the wire is that this is going to be the *Big-One*."

"Actually" Anna swept her hair back as she spoke, "It all sounds far *too* big for a sleepy little Sussex village."

"Drugs *are* big business everywhere today. Our information from Hong Kong is that the Triads are . . ."

"*Triads*?"

"The Hong Kong mafia."

"You can't possibly be serious Mr Lane?"

Wayne Lane waved a hand towards Chelsea-Ann.

"Police Officer Ferrari is the expert on the drug producing countries of the East. That's why she's here."

Anna turned to her "Is Mr Lane serious?"

"I'm afraid so. The whole of the Golden Triangle and Kuhn Sa in particular are . . ."

"Wait a minute." For the first time Anna spoke like a school mistress. "I don't know what you are talking about. Triads? Golden Triangle? and Coo . . . whatever it is?"

"Kuhn Sa. He is drug Warlord of the Shan States. The Golden Triangle is the point where China, Burma and Thailand meet. It is also where Kuhn Sa has his stronghold. He has a private army to protect his poppy fields, they stretch a thousand square miles on both sides of the River Salween, almost up to the Irrawaddy."

"You *are* both serious, aren't you?" Anna paled slightly at the realisation.

Wayne Lane smiled "We sure are, Miss Richardson, we sure are."

"Why don't the police search every piece of luggage that arrives at Gatwick and each boat that sails into the Channel. Wouldn't that stop it?"

"It isn't as easy as that." Chelsea-Ann spoke with authority. "Thailand is the world's largest exporter of rice. You should visit Bangkok and see the thousands of rice trucks on the roads every day, heading for the four points of the compass. And the hundreds of ships that leave for every known destination. That's before you start looking for suitcases with false bottoms, or search the inside of every exported television tube and every barrel of tripe. The best chance we have, is not to strip-search innocent tourists, but to smash every successful drug route. That's why we are in Kings Nympton.

Up to this point Mervyn had merely regarded Chelsea-Ann as the dumb brunette who accompanied

Wayne Lane. He now saw her as a police officer of some standing and one who knew her job. "Where in Kings Nympton exactly?", he asked.

She turned to Wayne Lane "Lieutenant?"

"Well our reports suggest Max Keating and his pub over there."

"We think that too."

Her anxiety was becoming tinged with guilt. Anna added "And I left Mike this morning when we realised that *The Slug and Lettuce* was involved."

"Do you think he went there by himself?"

"There is only one way to find out."

"You're right."

They crossed the Green to *The Slug and Lettuce* which had now closed for the afternoon. They knocked at the front door, the sound echoing through the building and hinting that the pub had been abandoned. The door was a heavy piece of ancient timber which would need a battering ram to dislodge it from its frame. So they went to the rear of the building. The requirements of the Health Inspector had meant that a new kitchen had been built onto the existing building and Mervyn hardly needed to put his shoulder to the door before it opened to let them in.

They found themselves in a modern kitchen gleaming with stainless steel and white tiles. An archway on the right led to a stairway giving access to the rooms above; Chelsea-Ann went in that direction. The others headed for the bar, pausing to look into the small store rooms on the way. They could hear Chelsea-Ann's footsteps as she searched the rooms above. The store rooms and bar were empty, so they headed back towards the kitchen and the archway that led to the staircase, meeting Chelsea-Ann as she descended.

"Nobody up there?"

"No."

"Not a thing down here either."

"Cellar?"

"Here's the door."

"And the light."

They clattered down the wide steps, dispersing at the bottom to search the separate bays. As their eyes became accustomed to the darkness, they made a thorough search.

"Just barrels of beer here."

"And cases of wine."

They moved back towards the centre area of the cellar where a naked light bulb hung from a loose fitting.

"Nothing."

"Not a thing."

Chapter 12

"The evidence upstairs indicates that the birds have flown." Chelsea-Ann spoke as soon as they had all climbed back to the kitchen.

"And we know there is going to be a drop tonight." Wayne Lane made a face, shrugged his shoulders and sighed. "But we don't know *when* and we don't know *where*."

"But we *do*." said Anna.

"Malcolm left a note" added Mervyn "It's tonight at eleven, on the Dragon's Back."

"The vicar says . . ." all eyes turned and focused on Anna "It's a Chinese way of saying it will be on the top of May Hill. He's *certain* it is."

"At eleven?"

"Yes."

"We knew you were asking questions, but we didn't expect you to find any answers." Wayne Lane made a fist with one hand and punched the open palm of the other, "Boy you're faster than Moody's goose."

"Moody's *goose*?"

"Don't ask me where it comes from. It's a way of saying that you were pretty quick." Wayne Lane chuckled to himself as he turned and picked up the phone to dial a number, "Hello . . . ? Yes . . . You had better give me Chief Superintendent Don Selkirk,

please ... That's right, Lieutenant Lane N.Y.P.D."
There was a pause. "Well try ... er ... Sergeant
Williams ... Percy Williams." There was another
pause. "Sergeant this is Lieutenant Lane. Yes ...
Hello. Listen, we are at *The Slug and Lettuce* ... I'll
explain later ... Max Keating and his wife have got
away. That is right ... The place is deserted. Could
you send someone to take charge of the building and
make it secure? And could you tell Chief Superintendent Selkirk. Yes I know he is out. Could you tell him
that the Keatings have gone. Now *this* is important,
it looks as if the drop is tonight at eleven o'clock....
Yes, twenty-three hundred ... on May Hill. O.K. Ask
him to call a briefing meeting for eight-thirty. We'll
be there. Bye now."

If anyone had watched Mervyn Lyle, over the last
few minutes, they would have witnessed a complete
transformation, as he changed from being Mervyn P.
Lyle into the knocker boy, who could wheedle a genuine Welsh Dresser from its owner and make him feel
that he was doing Mervyn a good turn by letting him
take it away for five pounds. This plausible, silver-
tongued huckster, now turned to Wayne Lane,
"Lieutenant?"

'Yes."

"We have just given you a vital piece of information."

"There is no doubt about that Mr Lyle."

"I would like to ask a favour in return?"

"Sure. What can I do?"

"I've been on the trail of these drug suppliers for
some days. I would like to be with you when you go
to May Hill tonight. I don't think the Brighton police
would allow that. So I'm asking you."

"Mmm. I guess you're right about your local police.
They're not sold on *glasnost* and *perestroika* in a big
way." Wayne Lane sighed, "On the other hand we

133

would have been helpless without your information.
Sure, you can ride in my car. But I will need your
word, as a gentleman, that you will stay in the car
and not get involved in any Police business. How about
that?"

"I'm not a gentleman, Lieutenant, but you can have
my word."

"O.K."

"Yeah."

When the cellar door was slammed shut and bolted
cutting Mike off into sudden darkness, his first feeling
was one of anger that he couldn't get up straightaway
and try to get out. But the ropes biting into his wrists
and ankles quickly banished the frustration, as a dull
throbbing ache began to drain his body and mind.
The effort expended in trying to free himself was so
strenuous that he toppled sideways and then didn't
have the leverage to heave himself upright again.
Lying on his side, he tugged and pulled at the ropes,
taking advantage of the floor to try and work the gag
from his mouth, but all to no avail. After some while
he was so exhausted that he gave up any further
attempt to free himself. The dwarfs may have been
rather short in stature, but they had used considerable
skill in securing him with two short pieces of rope.

He heard the first customers arriving upstairs in
the bar. Soon the noise was such that no one would
have heard a cry for help, even if he had been able to
make it. Surprisingly he could still pick out familiar
voices above the general sound of conversation.

Cramp, discomfort, and the darkness seemed to blur
the passing of time, although at one point he was
aware that the noise upstairs was getting thinner.
Eventually the door opened, the light came back on,
as Max and the dwarfs returned to the cellar. They

pulled him upright so that his back was once more against a wall.

"We're going to get you out of here, just in case."

Mike grunted. It was all he could do. The dust from the cellar floor and the gag had dried and parched his mouth and throat.

"Free his ankles, Bildad." Max turned to Mike. "There is no point in trying any funny business. These fellows have a remarkably silent way of keeping people quiet – they use pick-axe handles." He turned to the senior dwarf. "You bring up the rear. If he makes any hint of trying to run for it, *hit* him hard . . . and again if necessary."

"I could get to like that Mr Keating." The voice rasped from some fathomless depth. Mike was then bundled up the stairs. At first his legs didn't want to work. They felt numb and as if they didn't belong to him. The dwarf, with remarkable strength, kept him going through the kitchen and the back door into the garden. A path led through an overgrown orchard to a concealed shed at the far end of the property. Mike was pushed inside and his ankles retied. Max Keating lifted a pile of empty sacks from a corner and then one of the dwarfs must have hit him from behind. His next memory was the awareness of total silence and the pungent smell and the jute sacks, weighing heavily on his aching body. The sacking and dust tickled and aggravated the dryness of his throat.

A little after 8.30, Chief Superintendent Donald Selkirk, together with his aides and the two Americans, filed into the conference room of St John's Street Police Station in Brighton. It was full of police officers from the Brighton area, supplemented with men and women from the surrounding forces, who had been drafted in as back-up teams. Nearly all were in civilian dress and at the sight of their Commanding Officer, the joking and leg-pulling between various groups ceased.

Facing the gathering, at the front of the room, was a raised platform furnished with five empty chairs, four of these were now filled by the Chief Superintendent's party. He chose to remain standing, as he read a briefing document that had been handed to him as he came into the hall. Immediately behind him, pinned to a display board on the wall, was a large scale Ordnance Survey map of Kings Nympton and the area of Downs between the village and the sprawling conurbation of Brighton and Hove. To one side were two flip-chart easels, one holding a pad and the other an enlarged aerial photograph of May Hill.

Donald Selkirk looked up from the memo and put it at the bottom of the pile of papers in his hand. "Good evening. We have several things on our agenda. First, we need some background information. You won't know, that recent events in Hong Kong, have produced a war in Europe between the various gangs who want to supply drugs. Each gang wants to have its own patch of territory here in the West. I'm going to ask Police Officer Ferrari of the New York Police Department, to paint in the background details that she thinks are necessary."

There was a general murmur of approval from the men as Chelsea-Ann stood. The general view seemed to be that police women in New York were more glamourous than their counterparts in England. Chelsea-Ann crossed to the easel with the pad, picking up a red marker on the way.

"There are about fifty Triad gangs who are looking for territory and a role outside Hong Kong by 1997. Among them, are three major gangs that will interest you here in the U.K. Let me put their names on the board. You might find some of them amusing, so I ought to warn you that they all consist of extremely vicious men and women."

In spite of the warning, there was a titter as she wrote

SAM YEE ON
WO ON LOK
HUNG FAT SHAN
14K

"It is the *Sam Yee On* that you are dealing with in Sussex. They haven't had a base in England before, but over the past few months have been muscling their way in. The *Wo On Lok* have been in the U.K. since the 1930's and have had a very strong presence since the 1970's. Their main power base is in Manchester, although they do have a small patch of territory in London. It's on the west side, around Queensway. The *14K* are the dominant Soho gang. They came to Britain in 1975 and are an off-shoot of the *Hung Fat Shan*. They are called *14K* because originally, they used to meet at 14 Po Wah Road in Canton. Now are there any questions on the ground that I have covered so far?"

A young policeman in the second row raised a hand "You refer to gangs. How many members does each gang have?"

"I fear that *gang* is the wrong word, but it is the one we normally use. Perhaps a better word would be *family, tribe,* or *clan,* because the Triads aren't gangs in the way that we have street gangs in New York. The figures from observers reveal that 20% of the community in Hong Kong are members of one or other of the Triad groups. It is thought that in the U.K. at least one employee in every Chinese business is a member of a Triad gang. Many of these are *sleepers* but they can be activated very quickly by the gang's hierarchy. So we are dealing with big numbers. I've read one report here in England that describes the Triad gangs as a 'masonic movement with knives'. So they are very big. Does that answer your question?"

"Yes. Thank you. That's very helpful."

"Any more questions?"

A woman police officer towards the back of the meeting stood. "What you are saying is that one day, the majority of the drug business here will be run by the Triads?"

"No, I am putting it more strongly than that. I would say that the majority of business is theirs already. In Australia the Sydney Police Department, says that 70% of all high quality, uncut drugs come from a Triad source. What has happened previously, is that the Triads have used other people to do their business in the U.S. and Europe, but from now on, they're going to do it themselves. So, let me say it again – the majority of drugs from the East originate from Triad sources, they always have."

A Sergeant in the front row asked, "Are there any other sides to their business, apart from drugs?"

"That's a good question. They have three main bases for their business ventures; drugs, as we've already seen; gambling, where they specialise in *Maj Jong, Fan Tan* – that is roulette, and *Pai Kau* – that is dominoes. These last two sound pretty tame stuff, but the Chinese communities are dominated by gambling, so it's big business. The third interest of the Triads, is the video business. Again it sounds pretty trivial, but a major Hollywood movie can be pirated in Hong Kong and any market flooded with thousands of copies within days. This could make them six million dollars in a year, from just one movie."

"Are there any more questions? . . . O.K. I will conclude. I've duplicated a sheet of the Triad slang words. If you make any arrests tonight, it might be helpful to know one or two words in their *patois*."

One of the Chief Superintendent's aides started to circulate the paper.

"Notice the two Triad words for 'Policeman' at the top of the list. It's either *'Chut Chai'* which means 'Pawn' or *'Fa Yiu'* which means 'flowery waist'. So thanks a lot for listening you – *flowery waists*."

The meeting erupted into laughter and applause as Police Officer Chelsea-Ann Ferrari returned to her seat.

Chief Superintendent Selkirk rose to his feet. "I must say we are very grateful to our colleagues from New York, for their assistance. Background information, such as we have just been given, is immensely valuable. I confess, I knew little or nothing about the Triads until a few weeks ago." He turned to Chelsea-Ann, "Police Officer Ferrari thank you very much indeed." He swung back to the meeting, shuffling papers in his hand until he had the right page on top. "Now let me give you one or two pieces of information before Sgt. Metcalfe briefs you on tonight's operation."

"You are aware that we are dealing with a gang called the *San Yee On*. Their *modus operandi*, until recently, was to use couriers on scheduled flights from Hong Kong, to carry packages into this country. All of these contained a Chinese vase, copied from the K'ang Hsi period and which originated from one particular shop in Kowloon. The polystyrene matrix, that held the vase in place in its box for the journey, also contained half a kilo of high quality heroin. That amount may appear to be insignificant, so I should add that this was delivered on the daily flight to Gatwick. The package travelled here in a plastic carrier bag similar to thousands used in Hong Kong but with a clever colour code that enabled the courier to be spotted at Gatwick. He or she, would then be relieved of this extra piece of luggage on the Express to Victoria."

"Within the last week, an innocent holiday maker in Hong Kong purchased a K'ang Hsi vase from the shop in Kowloon. It was boxed, wrapped and placed in the wrong type of carrier bag – it was the type that the London connection were looking-out for. The passenger didn't take the Victoria train, he waited for a taxi which took him to the village where he lives. It was there that the package was taken from him by force. It would appear that it was only at that moment, that the gang realised their mistake."

"Our colleagues in Hong Kong have confirmed, that this particular method of transport has come to an end. Their enquiries show, that the operation was already being stepped up with larger deliveries to be made by freighter. These freighters will be intercepted in the Channel by helicopter, their sinister packages picked up mid-Channel, and delivered to a rendezvous in Sussex. It is such a delivery that we are expecting tonight. The customs are already shadowing the freighter involved. They will allow the helicopter to pick-up its consignment and deliver it to May Hill. Your job, is to apprehend the people involved, to immobilise the helicopter and, we hope, to arrest some senior members of the *San Yee On* gang. Thank you for your patience. Now let me hand over to Sgt. Metcalfe."

As the Chief Superintendent sat down there was a murmur of discussion in the hall. The Sergeant had to quieten the meeting before he could continue. "Just . . . just a few more moments quiet please. I won't keep you long and then we can all get on with tonight's work."

The Sergeant walked to the flip-chart easel with the aerial photograph of May Hill and picked up a marker. "This is the location where we are expecting everything to happen tonight. The only difference is that you will find a May-pole has been erected . . . here." He marked the position on the photograph. "Max

Keating, the publican of *The Slug And Lettuce*, has arranged a May Celebration as a diversion for the operation. The May-pole has already been decorated." The Sergeant added a few streamers to his drawing. "The brewery have put up a beer tent just about here." Again this was marked on the photograph. "Local Morris dancers have been engaged and there will be a Sword Dance Team coming from Yorkshire to put on a display. *This* is the road to Devil's Dyke." The Sergeant placed his index finger on the map. "It joins the A2038 and A281 and is really the main road from Brighton to Henfield. And just about here." The Sergeant pointed again, "is a small parking area looking over May Hill in one direction and the Devil's Dyke in the other. We have borrowed a mobile hamburger stand from the Met to be manned by Sergeant Percy Williams and W.P.C. Carol Semplar. It is already in place." The meeting erupted into cheers and clappings.

"Quiet please. There will be plenty of time to celebrate later, if we're successful. The hamburger stand is for all intents and purposes the genuine article, but it is also our Radio Car and the radio channel to HQ here in Brighton will always be open. If you need to get a message to us, simply go to the counter and speak, we'll pick it up. On the other hand, you could buy a hamburger which will keep your hunger at bay until you get back to the canteen. We'll consider reimbursing you for any necessary purchases," added the Sergeant allowing himself a small deviation from the written details in his notes.

At this point the Sergeant crossed to the Ordnance Survey map, picking up a Chinacraft pencil on the way and discarding the magic marker. "Sgt. Williams and W.P.C. Semplar will be here." He put an "x" on the map. "I want Group 'A' here in King's Wood. Those in Group 'B', please get to May Hill in your own transport and mix with the crowd. You will already have your instructions. Group 'C', the Task Force to immobilise the helicopter, you'll have to play it by ear. Try to spot the area which a helicopter might use and make your plans accordingly. There is a minibus for your use in the car park. The back-up teams, that is Groups 'D, E and F' will park their buses here." Again it was marked on the map.

"Are there any questions?" There was a pause, "Right, please check your watches. The time now is 8.52 and . . . 30 seconds. I want you all in position by 9.30. Good luck. Let's go for it."

Chapter 13

Earlier in the afternoon, as soon as the two Americans left, Mervyn had walked Anna to her car which she had left outside *The Den of Antiquity*. She unlocked the door, and as Mervyn held it open for her, suddenly something dawned on him, "Wa . . . ait a moment!"

Anna had smoothed the pleats of her skirt ready to get in, but let them go and waited for him to continue.

"This morning, Harry told me *where* he found the vases."

"Where?"

"An old shed at the bottom of the garden next door. He didn't want to say anything, because I am sure he stole them. Now if, and it's a *big* if, if Max Keating thought Mike was on to him, he might have shut him up, and hidden him in the shed. Nobody would ever think of looking there, because nobody knows it exists hidden among the trees. If Mike is not in the pub it is the only place he can be, otherwise Max would've had to take him through the village in broad daylight and somebody would have seen them."

"Let's go and have a look."

"Lets."

They walked back around the pub to the kitchen door which had been forced open earlier by Mervyn. It was still hanging slightly ajar, with the mortice part of the lock torn from the frame. They felt like trespassers, in spite of the fact that they knew *The Slug and Lettuce* was empty. They followed a path through overgrown vegetation and unpruned fruit trees. The shed was at the far end of the garden in a small copse and leaning precariously against a rotting fence. It looked as if it hadn't been used for years; black windows reflected the darkness of the orchard and cobwebs were just visible hanging inside, like disintegrating net curtains in a deserted slum. They tried the door, but it was locked.

Mervyn endeavoured to see inside, cupping his hands to stop the reflection. "Mm ... I don't think there is anything in there. Just a pile of old sacks. It isn't worth trying to get in. Let's leave it."

Anna caught his arm. "Someone has been down this path today." She pointed to broken and crushed vegetation and clods of earth that had been kicked up from the path. "And if there is nothing in the shed, why lock it?"

"Perhaps you are right." Mervyn reluctantly put his shoulders to the door, the rotting wood collapsed easily and noiselessly under his weight.

The light from the opened door revealed Mike's feet, which was all he had managed to free as he kicked the sacks in an effort to escape. Anna and Mervyn pulled the rest away from him.

"Hey we've found you," Mervyn said as he tore the gag from Mike's mouth.

Mike spluttered for a moment, then said hoarsely "I didn't expect you to find me. I was sure no one knew about this shed."

"Harry told me this morning this was where he found the vases. Hang on a moment I need my knife. Whoever tied you up knew what they were doing. Was it Max?"

"No the dwarfs."

"*The* dwarfs?"

"Yes, they work for him."

"Y'kidding? Hey – keep still and we'll soon have you free." Mervyn sawed at the ropes that held Mike's hands behind his back. The last strand severed with a thud-like sound. "There you are." Mike was free.

They helped him to his feet and he hobbled around for a few moments. "My legs have gone to sleep." He took a deep breath noisily through his teeth and clutched at Mervyn for support. "I'll be all right in a moment." He shook his hands to restore the circulation in his wrists.

They waited for him to speak.

Eventually he said "Felix Platter was one of Max's ancestors and now he has become his role model. Before *The Slug and Lettuce* was a pub, it once belonged to Felix. He used the cellars for contraband, as well as a network of dwarfs. Now Max wants to be like Felix and his emulation has gone as far as having a band of dwarfs too."

"They're bodyguards d'mean?"

"No – more than that. They're his couriers. Max's part in the organisation was to collect the money. Apparently his business 'front' in London, was some sort of circus agency. The dwarfs travelled across Europe using circuses as their cover, and brought the money back to London. Once Max was sure it couldn't be traced, he banked it in Guernsey."

"If the dwarfs are so important, why haven't we seen more of them." Anna frowned.

"Because Max has been careful to keep the organisation's business away from Kings Nympton. In the village, he just likes to be known as the publican. But now everything is being closed down and there are only three dwarfs left. They leave tonight, with Max, after the final delivery."

"How did you find all this out?" said Anna, still frowning.

"Max is proud of it. He almost boasts about it. He told me everything when he and the dwarfs brought me here earlier."

"He must be mad."

"He is definitely a psychopath . . ." Mike was going to continue.

"Oh." Anna raised her hands to stop him. "Mervyn was right about the Americans. They are police officers – Drug Squad from New York. I only hope they are good enough to catch Max and 'Ma' – and the dwarfs."

"Well Max is coming back tonight for the last delivery." Mike shrugged and raised his hands in despair. "But the only trouble is, we don't know where it is going to be."

"Yes we do," said Anna. "It's on the top of May Hill. That's what Malcolm's note said. It's Chinese – the vicar told us." She glanced at Mervyn and then back to Mike. "You won't believe this, but Mervyn has got permission from the Lieutenant to be in the back of his car tonight."

"Have you now," said Mike with a smile.

Mike's pallor reminded Anna of the ordeal from which he was only just escaping and said "I think we should get you home."

"What a good idea. A cup of tea and a hot bath should sort out my dry throat and aching limbs." They headed back across the Green towards his cottage.

As Wayne Lane's car sped out of Brighton the colour of the night sky changed from bright sodium orange to a deep velvety indigo, finally fading to a cold blue moonlight. The eerie light bathed the Downs, transforming them into an enormous sleeping animal. The car dropped towards Kings Nympton with the Devil's Dyke on one side and on the other, May Hill rising above the sylvan blackness of King's Wood. The dark tracery of the taller trees etched the night sky to the east.

As they followed the bend in the road, they suddenly found themselves caught up in the noise and bustle of the *May Celebration*. At first sight it looked like a medieval carnival. Flames leapt into the air from huge wrought iron torches. The vicar was roasting a side of beef and selling generously filled sandwiches in aid of St Rumon's building fund. Behind him, the beer tent with one open side, revealed a makeshift bar served by a team of young people who seemed unable to cope with the crowd who pressed forward with their orders. Immediately in front of the parking area and overlooking the whole scene was Sgt. William's hamburger stand. He and W.P.C. Semplar were doing a roaring trade. The cars parked on the Devil's Dyke side of the road, stretched down almost as far as Kings Nympton.

High on May Hill a group of nymphs decked with garlands of spring flowers, danced the ancient rustic rite around the May pole. They must have been the girl friends of the regulars at the *Snooty Fox*, because it was the young fogies from Wilmington, who encouraged them with Bacchanalian choruses of familiar Rugby songs.

The air was full of music and the sound of people enjoying themselves.

Wayne Lane's car came to a halt just past the hamburger stand. He turned to Mike and Anna wedged with Mervyn on the back seat, "We're late I'm afraid. Forgive me. I had to fax a long report to the U.S. Chelsea-Ann, would you mind parking the car at the bottom of the hill?" Turning back towards the rear seat. "Now because we can't stay here I am not going to ask you to remain in the car; you may get out enjoy yourselves, please remember not to get in the way of the police."

The three scrambled from the car and into the crowd that filled the parking area. The *Barnsley Long-sword Dance Side* were getting ready to "dance out" a display in a roped off square. They were dressed in red and white caps, white shirts, black breeches and red stockings. From the sidelines a James Robertson Justice figure, in an Inverness Cape, took a Meerschaum pipe from his mouth and called "Rattle up my boys". The dancers rehearsed their final "locking" movement in which six swords emerged from a scrum as a single hexagonal symbol held aloft by the leader. The swords, reflecting the flames of the torches, stood out against the night sky like a large fiery *Star of David*.

Elsewhere in the crowd, were top hatted groups of Morris Dancers, dressed in white and wearing waistcoats alive with flying rectangles of colour. Their legs, decorated with gaudy garters and bells, leaped to the pipe and tabor with handkerchiefs waving from their hands to the same rhythm.

Above the cacophony and general gaiety of the scene, it would have been easy to miss the first faint, th-thud . . . th-thud . . . th-thud . . . th-thud . . . above the other sounds. But then with slightly more noise and a flashing light a Lynx helicopter came into view above the Downs. It hovered for a moment to find its bearing, then with a huge down draft, it swept to an area next to the car park, gently settling on the ground.

Three dwarfs appeared out of the shadows. They were immediately overcome by, what a few moments earlier had appeared to be a group of inebriated rustics, but who had become a very efficient police snatch-squad.

A similar team went for the helicopter. One seemed to clamber up on the fuselage and place something near the base of the rotor blades. After a few seconds there was a flash and a C-R-U-M-P, followed by a ball of smoke rising in the air. The helicopter's engine spluttered and died, whereupon the pilot was hauled smartly from one side and Max Keating from the other. Both were hand-cuffed and led to the road where a police car screeched to its position and drove them away.

Nearer the road another group of police had rounded up three or four young Chinese including the young man that Mike and Anna had seen in the *Taiping Supermarket*. They were whisked away in a minibus. The whole operation, from the first appearance of the helicopter to the final arrest, barely lasted five minutes and had been conducted with surgical precision.

A police car with a flashing blue light came down the hill and halted near the hamburger stand receiving a nod of acknowledgement from Sgt. Williams. Chief Superintendent Donald Selkirk emerged and strode to the high point of the parking area. Using a loud-hailer he announced "Ladies and Gentlemen, we have had to do a little police business here this evening. I am glad to say it is over now and it has been achieved without any injuries. I am assigning a guard for the helicopter until the low-loader arrives, apart from that, we are going to leave you in peace. Enjoy your evening. Thank you." Donald Selkirk walked quickly back to his car and was driven off with his aides.

Mike was about to suggest to Anna that they might walk back to Kings Nympton and use his car to drive to Brighton to retrieve hers, when Wayne Lane and Chelsea-Ann Ferrari appeared from the crowd. The Lieutenant was first to speak. "Well, mission accomplished Mr Main. I heard on the radio that they have arrested the Keatings and have also picked up some of the 'key' members of the *San Yee On* gang. It has been a successful night's work, for which we must thank Mr Lyle and Miss Richardson because they told us about the er . . . how do the Chinese put it . . . ?"

"The Dragon's Back."

" 'The Dragon's Back' yes, of course, thank you." Wayne Lane turned towards Mervyn, "Mr Lyle you can rest now, knowing that the dealers who supplied your sister are under lock and key. It won't bring her back, but I think we can promise that they will be out of circulation for a long time."

"Thank you Lieutenant."

"You're welcome. Now let's get you folks back to Brighton."

Mike turned with an enquiring glance to Anna and then to Wayne Lane, "I think we'll get back under our own steam. If that's all right?"

"Sure. That's fine." He held out his hand, "Mr Main, it's been a real privilege meeting with you. I am sorry we deceived you. But I spoke the truth about food. Food *really* is my hobby. I will never forget the meal at *The Old Nail Shot*. A gourmet feast. I'll just run Mr Lyle back then."

They all shook hands and said "Good bye." Wayne Lane, Chelsea-Anne and Mervyn moved off to look for their car. The police activity had dampened the festive spirit which couldn't be recaptured. Only the truly committed pursued their dancing and drinking as if nothing had happened but those who had come out of curiosity drifted away down the hill in search of their cars.

As Mike and Anna walked towards Kings Nympton they were overtaken by a group of clog-dancers in flat caps, black trousers and waistcoats. They were skipping and hopping their way down Kissing Tree Lane. It was only when they had passed that Mike and Anna realised that the last dancer, dressed in denim and without a flat cap, was in fact Hallelujah Harry. Somehow, he had acquired clogs and was keeping perfect time with the *Chester Clog-Dancers*. The back of his denim jacket said "*Sea Sharp Shanty Band*".

The vicar also hurried past them down the hill, but stopped and raised his hat when he saw them. "Ah g . . . good evening to both of you."

"Did you enjoy that?" Anna peered enquiringly around Mike towards him.

"The er . . . Clog dancers?"

"No the May Celebration."

"Oh it can be very d . . . dangerous, you know? In this part of S . . . Sussex there is evidence of a very old and primitive religion. Any return to that, must be resisted. I certainly don't think it should be encouraged among the young. They aren't often aware that when they dance around the May pole, they are actually worshipping a pagan god."

"I thought you would've liked all the old customs and ceremonies?"

"When they are harmless that, of course, is a d . . . different matter. Most of the events tonight had no real connection with S . . . Sussex. There is evidence that May Hill was once used for a fertility rite. You see, it is the connection with sex that is being exploited; that's what attracts the young. But they are being seduced by a very dark and evil force, and I don't think they understand that. It all goes to what the Greeks called *Ge* and the Romans *Tellus* – Mother Earth – a goddess of the nether world." The vicar paused thoughtfully for a moment. "Actually, in the last three hundred years, the big day locally wasn't May 1st, but the 29th. In this part of Sussex it is always known as *Pinch-Bum Day*."

"Sorry?"

"Pinch-Bum Day. Yes, that is what I said, traditionally the children wear an oak apple or an oak leaf pinned to their clothes. The penalty for not 'Sporting their oak' was having their legs slashed with stinging nettles. In Brighton, a pinch on the bottom was the punishment – hence the local name. The May 29th was the birthday of Charles II and also the day he returned in 1660, to claim his throne. The pinching was in memory of the time when he hid in an oak tree at Boscobel, after the Battle of Worcester. You perhaps remember a Colonel Careless had to keep pinching the King on that spot, to prevent him from falling asleep and therefore out of the tree."

"Another delightful piece of history," Anna smiled. "You're a mine of information, vicar."

"Useless information that has no relevance for today – I fear. I was *wrong* about the dwarfs wasn't I? I had a w . . . word with a policeman on May Hill." The vicar pointed up the hill into the darkness. "He told me that they've arrested the Keatings and the dwarfs. So you *were* right; the two things were connected. Who would have thought that such nice people as the Keatings would be involved with drugs. That is what they are saying, you know . . . drugs . . . a very nasty business. I gather we were *all* under suspicion. Did you know that?"

"Well *we* . . ." Anna blushed when she realised that she couldn't possibly say that they had thought the vicar was involved.

"I know what you are going to say," the vicar spoke quickly, "It has to do with me saying that my previous parish was in the north?"

"Y . . . yes."

"I wasn't very convincing and I shouldn't have said it. You see, I was divorced about five years ago. As a clergyman I truly believe that marriage is for life. Yet sometimes it can go wrong even for a vicar . . . well mine did. Both my job as a clergyman and my interest in the flora and fauna of Sussex, upset my first wife and so she left me and eventually divorced me. Then I met Beryl; who shares all my interests . . . such a wonderful woman," the vicar paused, "It's not right that man should be alone. Now the government have changed the law, the Bishop has given me another chance with a parish, but I shouldn't have tried to deceive you. That was quite wrong. That's what made you suspect me wasn't it?"

"Yes. Thank you for being so frank."

"No. Thank you for being so understanding. You wouldn't know it but recently so much of me has changed. Some of the young men in the parish have been taking me to a church in the City. It has changed my attitude to everything. I wish I had had that sort of teaching when I was training to be a clergyman. My faith has been renewed – that's what has happened. Even my interest in Sussex is now going to take second place." He turned to Anna and beamed. "I think I might start to like preaching too. Things must be biblical, you know – they *must* be biblical."

The vicar suddenly seemed lost in thought and in an absent minded way said "Goodnight to you." He then turned and took the footpath that led down through the churchyard to the village. He was muttering to himself, "He logos gar ho stauros tois men appollumenois moria estin, tois sozomenois hemin dunamis Theou estin."

"Goodnight," called Anna to the vanishing figure.

"Goodnight and I'll look out for you on Tuesday," added Mike.

Mike and Anna watched the vicar go down the path. "Are you really going to the City church on Tuesday?"

"Yes," Mike also appeared to be lost in thought, "I am. The conversation we had on the train, settled it for me. Music is important – so is art. And in a different way – so is food. But without some sort of explanation of what we are doing here on earth – life's a bit like an engine running on one cylinder. I want to find the answer – so I'm going to join the young men from Lloyd's for study each week and they're going to take me to the church on Tuesday. It fits in with my day off, which is marvellous."

The lane was empty now and they walked in silence for a few moments. It was still just possible to hear the sound of what was left of the May Celebration on the top of May Hill.

They passed the entrance to the Manor. It was in darkness; Major Bradford must have retired, or had gone away for the night to escape the noise. A large cloud moved away from the moon, spotlighting the two badgers, about thirty yards ahead, out for a nocturnal stroll. Again, as they kept close to the bank at the side of the road, they leant towards each other. "It is easy for them," thought Anna. While Mike thought of the vicar's "It is not right for man to be alone."

He suddenly stopped in the middle of the road, and turned to Anna, "I am not looking forward to you going back to Roedean. You have come to mean a lot to me in the last few days, I think I'm in love with you."

"Oh, Mike, are you sure? Can you trust your feeling for me? After all, it's only a few months since Claire died."

He took her in his arms, intent on asking her to marry him, but found himself lost for words. The clouds moved back across the moon, like a curtain on a winter's evening, drawn to shut out the world, and its many pressing demands.

"I love you too, Mike," she responded as they embraced.

Despite the demands of life, they both knew they were free to enjoy the warmth of the growing love they were beginning to find in each other.

For Mike new waves of tenderness flooded into the barrenness of the long days without Claire – they were more than consolation, they were signs of new life – life to be lived to the full.